U0600375

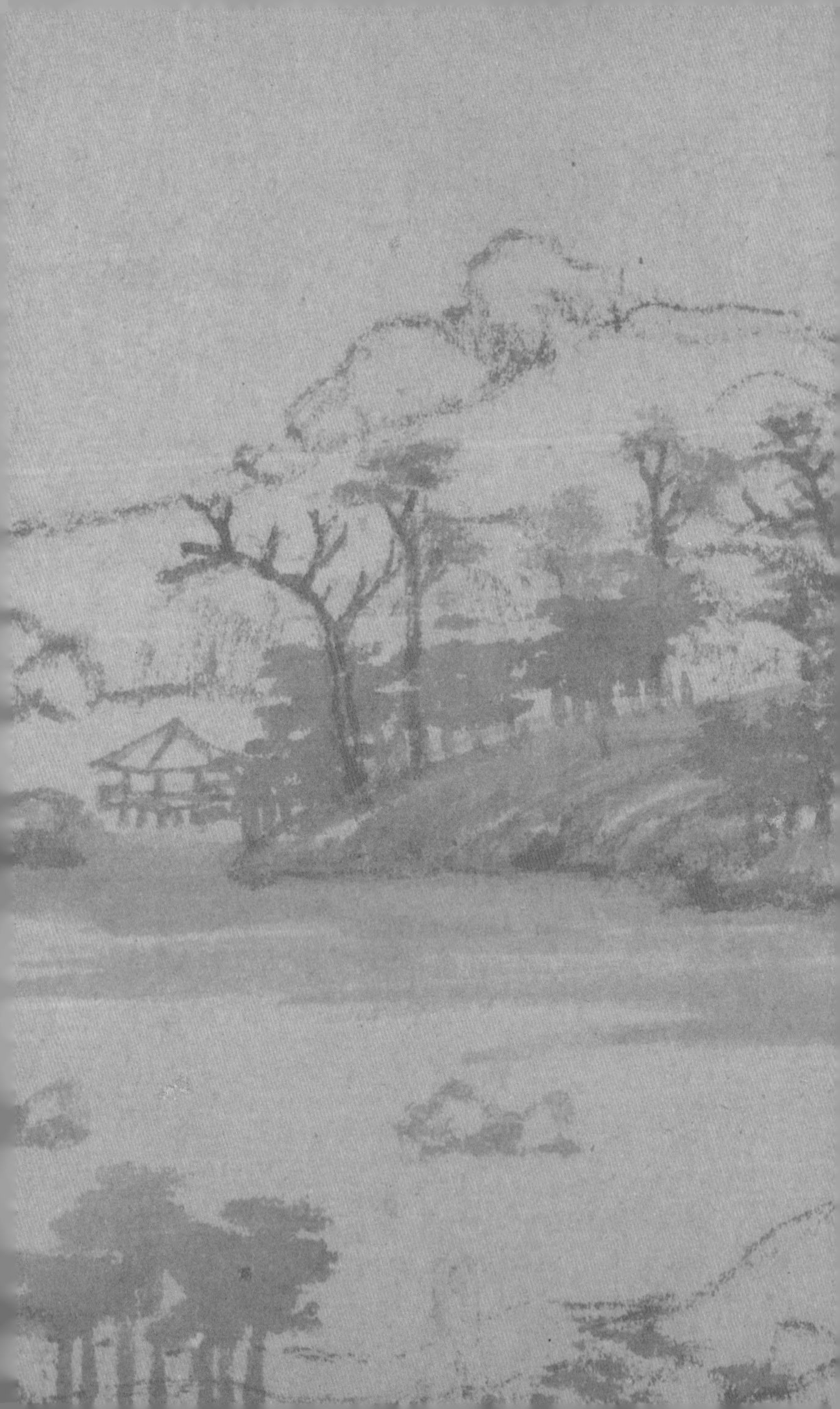

锦里繁华

汉英对照

美得窒息的宋词

许渊冲——译

吴佚阳——解析

长江出版传媒 | 长江文艺出版社

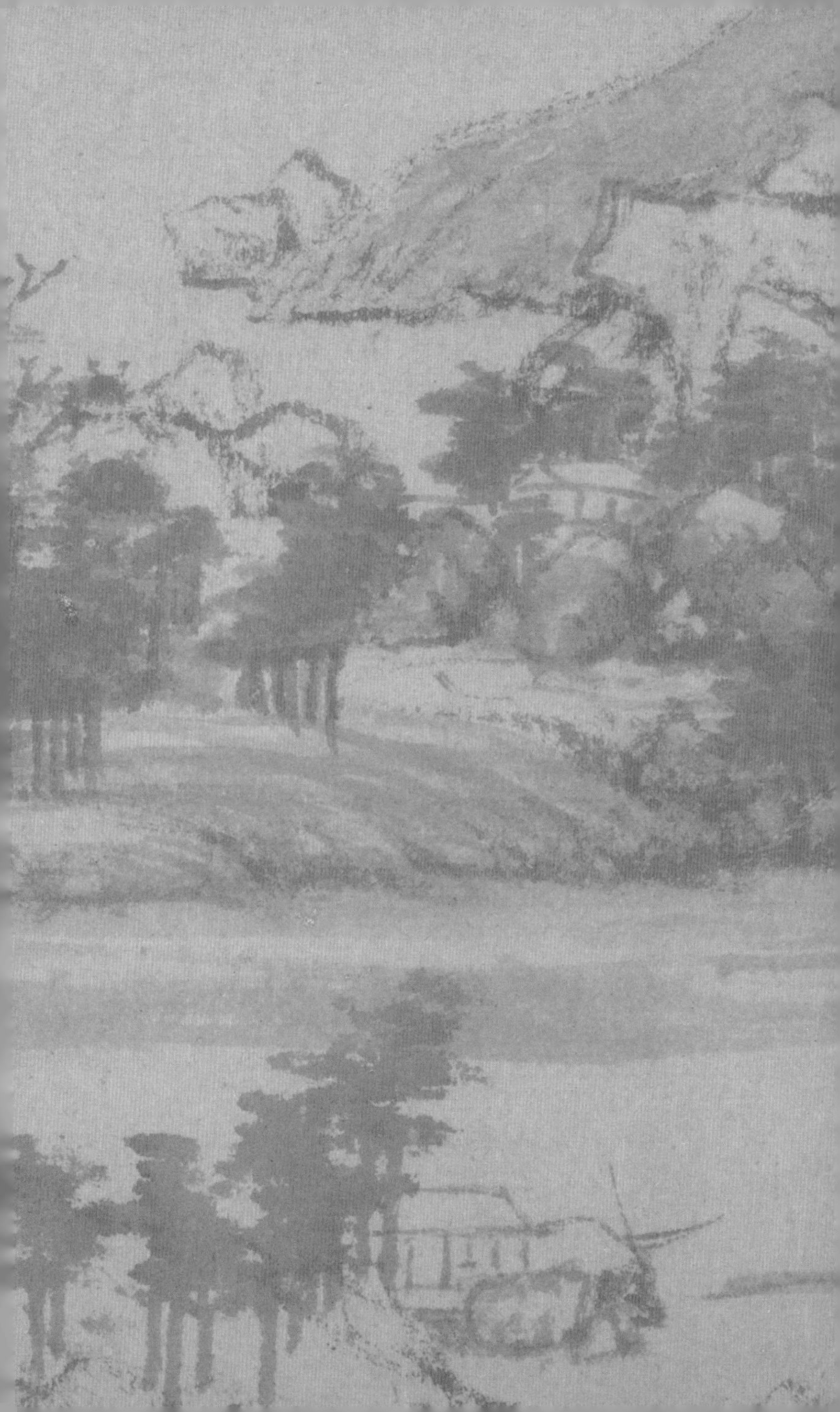

锦里繁华

美得窒息的宋词

许渊冲 译
吴俣阳 解析

汉英对照

长江出版传媒
长江文艺出版社

目录

Contents

第一章……烟柳画桥

第二章……红笺无色

第三章 …… 雨荷烟柳

第四章 …… 清愁自醉

第五章……山河故人

第六章……远山沧海

第一章

烟柳×画桥

CHAPTER ONE

The smokelike willows form a windproof screen

乳燕飞·波影摇涟甃 周密

辛未首夏，以书舫载客游苏湾，徙倚危亭，极登览之趣。所谓浮玉山、碧浪湖者，皆横陈于前，特吾几席中一物耳。遥望具区，渺如烟云，洞庭、缥缈诸峰，矗矗献状，盖王右丞、李将军著色画也。松风怒号，暝色四起，使人浩然忘归。慨然怀古，高歌举白，不知身世为何如也。溪山不老，临赏无穷，后之视今，当有契余言者。因大书山楹，以纪来游。

波影摇涟甃（zhòu）。趁熏风、一舸来时，翠阴清昼。去郭轩楹（yíng）才数里，藓（xiǎn）磴（dèng）松关云岫。快屐齿筇（qióng）枝先后。空半危亭堪聚远，看洞庭缥缈争奇秀。人自老，景如旧。来帆去棹还知否。问古今、几度斜阳，几番回首？晚色一川谁管领，都付雨荷烟柳。知我者、燕朋鸥友。笑拍阑干呼范蠡（lǐ），甚平吴、却倩垂纶手？吁万古，付卮（zhī）酒。

Nursling Swallows' Flight

Zhou Mi

The stone bank's shadows shake in the waves of the lake;
In summer breeze a boat comes near
When the green shade at noon is clear.
A few miles away from the city wall,
Over mossy lanes and pine-clad hills clouds veil all.
With boots on foot and cane in hand,
We can see in mid-air the pavilion stand
With a far-flung view to command.
See floating peaks in beauty vie,
Marvels under the sky.
In vain have oldened men;
The scene's the same as then.

Do you not know boats come and go
Now as long,long ago?
How many times has the sun set?
How many things not to forget?
Who would now enjoy the beautiful evening scene?
None but lotus in rain and mist-veiled willow green.
Who are my friends who know me?
Only the gulls and swallows keep me company.
Laughing and beating on the rail,
I ask General Fan to what avail
He had conquered the Northern land?
Now he had only a fishing line in hand.
Days pass by,rain or shine;
I'd drink a cup of wine.

宋度宗咸淳七年（1271年）的夏天，我以书舫载着客人，一起游于湖州乌程县南的苏湾，后又徒步爬上山顶的雄跨亭，极得登览之乐。浮玉山、碧浪湖，一一呈现在前，就像我案几上摆放的物件一样渺小。放眼望去，洞庭山、缥缈峰，无不高耸入云，像极了王维和李思训笔下的泼墨山水画，美得无与伦比。日暮时分，松林间风声大作，天色变得愈来愈晦暗，可我的兴致竟愈来愈高，到了乐不思归的地步。我们一边举着酒杯喝着美酒，一边缅怀着古人，不知身世究为何物。江山不老，登临游览，赏兴无穷，今后若有人来，当知我所言非虚，并因此特意书写在用山石凿成的石柱上，以为纪念。

碧波荡漾的湖面上，石砌的堤壁倒映在水中，形成了摇曳不定的光影，煞是好看。趁着这醉人的熏风，我们划着一叶轻舟穿梭在苏湾中，岸边翠绿的树荫更为我们挡住了炎炎夏日的滚滚热浪，让我们倍感清凉与惬意。

离开县城南关不过才数里地，触目所及之处，却已充满了野逸之趣。苔藓密布的山径石阶，道旁对列如关门的古松，白云舒卷下的苍山远峰，一切的一切，无不让人顿觉心旷神怡。我们穿着木屐，拄着筇枝所制的手杖，先后快步登上山，一心只想沿着山径寻胜访幽。

登上高耸于山崖之上的危亭，凭栏远眺，所有的景致都于一瞬间收聚于眼底。凝眸，太湖水浩浩荡荡，波光潋滟，洞庭山与缥缈峰浮沉于浪涛之间，宛若仙境，此情此景，自是美不胜收，妙不可言。

溪山不老，景物如旧，却叹人生短暂，倏忽间便已老去了许多年华，恰似那昙花一现、白驹过隙，怎不惹人惆怅意难平。眼前往来穿梭的船只，像极了世间追名逐利的营蝇狗苟之辈，他们又可曾知道，古往今来，岁月总是如流水般逝去，所有的人事变迁，也无非只是几度斜阳、几番回首罢了！

天色向晚，谁能统领这一片青山秀水的殊胜之美，恐怕也只有那雨中之荷、烟中之柳了。登临揽胜，日暮忘归，暂作湖山之主，自是赏心悦目，快活得忘乎所以，但这世间能够真正懂得我的又有几人呢？知我者，也不过就剩下同行的这几个朋友，还有翩翩飞过头顶的燕子与湖鸥了。

谈笑风生中，我兀自拍打着栏杆，大声呼唤着早已隐居在太湖之畔的越国大夫范蠡，想要借他这双垂钓的手，像帮助越王勾践灭亡吴国一样，将元军彻底赶出中原大地，还我大好河山。唉，说一千，道一万，在这里感叹万古流长，又有什么意义，还不如把一切离愁，都付于一杯酒中的好。

这阕词为词人与友人同游湖州乌程苏湾时所作。时值宋度宗咸淳七年，南宋灭亡在即。词人面对黑暗动荡的社会现状，虽满腹忧虑和不满，但又无能为力，便与张枢、杨缵等词友，时常往来嬉游于临安、湖州的青山绿水之间，借以逃避现实，并写下了大量优美的纪游抒情词，但情调大多颇为消极。

周密（1232 年—约 1298 年），字公谨，号草窗，又号四水潜夫、弁阳老人、华不注山人等。原籍济南，后为吴兴（今浙江省湖州市）人。南宋文学家。

南宋德祐年间，曾任义乌令等职，宋亡后隐居不仕。其词讲求格律，风格在姜夔、吴文英两家之间，与吴文英（梦窗）并称“二窗”，亦曾写过一些慨叹宋室覆亡之作。

能诗文善书画，谙熟宋代掌故。著有《草窗韵语》《齐东野语》《武林旧事》《癸辛杂识》《志雅堂杂钞》《云烟过眼录》《浩然斋雅谈》等，另编有《绝妙好词》。今存词一百五十余首。

望海潮·东南形胜

柳永

东南形胜，三吴[1]都会，钱塘自古繁华。烟柳画桥，风帘翠幕，参差十万人家。云树绕堤沙，怒涛卷霜雪，天堑（qiàn）无涯。市列珠玑，户盈罗绮，竞豪奢。重湖叠巘（yǎn）清嘉，有三秋桂子，十里荷花。羌管弄晴，菱歌泛夜，嬉嬉钓叟（sǒu）莲娃。千骑拥高牙，乘醉听箫鼓，吟赏烟霞。异日图将好景，归去凤池夸。

①三吴一作：江吴

Watching the Tidal Bore

Liu Yong

Scenic splendor southeast of River Blue
And capital of ancient Kingdom Wu,
Qiantang's as flourishing as e'er.
The smokelike willows form a windproof screen;
Adorned with painted bridges and curtains green,
A hundred thousand houses spread out here and there.
Upon the banks along the sand,
Cloud-crowned trees stand.
Great waves roll up like snowbanks white;
The river extends till lost to sight.
Jewels and pearls at the Fair on display,
Satins and silks in splendid array,
People vie in magnificence
And opulence.

The lakes reflect the peaks and towers,
Late autumn fragrant with osmanthus flowers,
Lotus in bloom for miles and miles.
Northwestern pipes play with sunlight;
Water chestnut songs are sung by starlight;
Old fishermen and maidens young all beam with smiles.
With flags before and guards behind you come;
Drunken, you may listen to flute and drum,
Chanting the praises loud
Of the land beneath the cloud.
You may picture the scene another day
And boast to the Court where you'll go in full array.

杭州地处东南要冲，风光秀丽，是三吴地区的都会，自古以来就十分繁华。放眼望去，到处都是如烟的柳树，彩绘的桥梁，雅致的风帘，翠绿的帐幕，楼阁高高低低，大约总计有十万户人家住在这里。

高耸入云的大树环绕着钱塘江沙堤，汹涌澎湃的潮水卷起霜雪一样洁白的浪花，宽广的江面一望无涯。市场上陈列着琳琅满目的珠玉珍宝，家家户户都贮存了大量的绫罗绸缎，争相比试着谁比谁更加豪奢。

里湖、外湖，还有灵隐、南屏那些重重叠叠的山岭，看上去都显得非常清秀可爱。秋天有飘香的桂花，夏天有逶迤十里的荷花，怎不让人爱煞了这座古老的城池。白天，人们在湖边欢快地吹奏羌笛；晚上，人们兴高采烈地划着船儿采着红菱唱着悦耳动听的歌，钓鱼的老翁和采莲的姑娘们，个个都喜笑颜开。

成群列队的骑兵，簇拥着高矗的军旗缓缓而来，声势显赫，谁都知道，那是杭州的父母官孙何要出巡了。听说这位官人不仅喜欢饮酒作乐，还是个艺术天才，时常在微醺中，一边听着箫鼓管弦，一边吟诗作词，毫不吝惜笔墨地赞赏这美丽的湖光山色。想必他日，这官人被召还京师之际，也一定会把这幅美好的景致用图画描绘出来，一一夸示于同僚，谓世间果真存有如此这般的人间仙境。

陈元靓《岁时广记》卷三十一引杨湜《古今词话》："柳耆卿与孙相何为布衣交。孙知杭州，门禁甚严。耆卿欲见之不得，作《望海潮》词，往谒名妓楚楚曰：'欲见孙相，恨无门路。若因府会，愿借朱唇歌于孙相公之前。若问谁为此词，但说柳七。'中秋府会，楚楚宛转歌之，孙即日迎耆卿预坐。"从这个故事来看，这阕词当是一首干谒词，目的是请求孙何向朝廷举荐自己。

柳永（约 987 年—约 1053 年），原名三变，字景庄，后改名柳永，字耆卿，因排行第七，又称柳七。崇安（今福建省南平市武夷山）人，生于沂州费县（今山东省费县）。北宋著名词人，婉约派杰出的代表人物。

二郎神·七夕

柳永

炎光谢。过暮雨、芳尘轻洒。乍露冷风清庭户，爽天如水，玉钩遥挂。应是星娥嗟久阻，叙旧约、飙biāo轮欲驾。极目处、微云暗度，耿耿银河高泻。

闲雅。须知此景，古今无价。运巧思、穿针楼上女，抬粉面、云鬟huán相亚。钿合金钗私语处，算谁在、回廊影下。愿天上人间，占得欢娱，年年今夜。

The Junior God
The Double Seventh Eve

Liu Yong

The heat will abate
After the evening rain,
Light fragrance and wet dust remain.
Cold turns the dew,
The breeze freshens the courtyard in view.
In the water-clear sky
A hooklike moon hangs high.
Hindered for long, the Weaving Maid sighs,
Now she may go on a date,
Driving her winged wheels in flight.
As far as she stretches her eyes,
She sees fleecy clouds rise
Over the Silver River bright.

Such rendezvous is priceless since old days.
A maiden comes downstairs
To thread a needle in clever ways,
Looking upward, her cloudlike hairs
Caress her powdered face.
Who in the corridor whispers in the shade?
It's her friend and his maid,
Exchanging golden hairpin and silver case.
They wish lovers may unite
Every year as this night
On earth as in the sky.

难耐的暑热终于消退了，暮雨过后，尘土为之一扫而空。刚结露的时候，冷风清理了庭院，抬头望望，碧空如水，一弯新月静静地挂在遥远的天边，好一个秋高气爽、温婉澄澈的夜晚，而这一切，似乎都是为牛郎织女一年一度的鹊桥相会所准备的。

兴许是织女嗟叹久与丈夫分离，为叙旧约，她驾着御风而行的车轮，迅速飞渡银河，直奔牛郎而去。触目所及之处，淡淡的云彩，在不知不觉中慢慢飘过银河，而那闪烁发亮、星光璀璨的银河，更是高高地悬挂在天际，仿佛要从天上流泻到人间一样。

没有繁盛宏大的场面，也没有喧闹热烈的气氛，家家户户都列于庭户乞巧望月，好一派闲静幽雅的景象。要知道，此情此景，古往今来，是多少钱也买不来的，若不珍惜这如梦的佳期，便是人生中最大的损失。

闺楼上的姑娘们，无一例外地在月光下抬起娇艳的粉面，无比虔诚地举起七孔针和各种彩线，手脚麻利地穿针引线，向织女乞取着巧艺，乌云般美丽的发髻都向后垂了下来，也没有察觉。猜猜，又是谁在回廊的影子下，窃窃私语着交换信物？欸，还是别猜了吧，唯愿天上人间，每年的七夕夜，都有这无尽的欢颜与永恒的喜悦。

这是一阕吟咏七夕佳期的词作。词人一反以往七夕诗词的伤感情调，用心地描摹出了一幅欢乐祥和、温馨甜美的七夕夜色图，并发出了珍惜良宵、莫负美景的呼唤，抒发了对纯真爱情的美好祝愿与热烈向往。全词语言通俗易懂，形象鲜明生动，情调清丽典雅，给人以充分的艺术享受。

风流子·新绿小池塘

周邦彦

新绿小池塘，风帘动、碎影舞斜阳。羡金屋去来，旧时巢燕；土花缭绕，前度莓墙。绣阁里、凤帏深几许？听得理丝簧。欲说又休，虑乖芳信；未歌先咽，愁近清觞shāng。遥知新妆了，开朱户，应自待月西厢。最苦梦魂，今宵不到伊行。问甚时说与，佳音密耗，寄将秦镜，偷换韩香？天便教人，霎时厮见何妨。

Song of Gallantry

Zhou Bangyan

The little pond is newly greened;
The breeze ruffles the window screened.
The broken shadows dance with slanting sunny rays.
I envy swallows flying to and fro
Under the eaves of golden hall,
And rampant flowers creeping high and low
Upon the age-old earthen wall.
I hear in curtained tower deep she plays
And vibrates zither strings.
She stops before she says anything,
She'd not betray her spring.
She sobs before she sings,
So sad as to decline
A cup of sweetest wine.

I know that after making up her face
She'd open crimson doors and pace
To view the moon from western bower.
It grieves me most tonight
That I can't bring fresh shower for the thirsting flower.
When will she tell me with delight
The time for us to meet?
When may I send her mirror bright
And she in turn her incense sweet?
O Heaven! O what harms
If I stay a while in her arms!

碧绿的春水涨满了小小的池塘，微风轻轻吹动纱帘，那破碎的帘影缓缓落于水面，在斜阳的映照下，显得格外的灵动可爱。

真羡慕那些可以在金屋里飞来飞去的燕子啊，它们又在旧年筑巢的梁上筑起了新巢，比神仙还要快活逍遥；还有那苍翠欲滴的苔藓，在前番生过的围墙上，又绕着院落再度萌发生长。

张挂着锦绣的闺房里，那华丽的帷帐究竟有多深？我只能听到从房中缓缓传出的丝竹之声，悠扬，缠绵，婉转，那曲调里仿佛蕴藏着许多欲说还休的心事，大概是担心错过了幽会的佳期，歌未出口，先已哽咽，便只好举起酒杯，借酒浇愁。

远远地望着她闺阁的方向，我知道，佳人已经梳理好了新妆，推开了窗户，怕是要一直守候在西厢的月光下，默默等待着我的到来。最苦涩而又无奈的是，因有公务缠身，今夜里，纵是在梦中，灵魂也无法抵达她的身边。

问何时，才能向她倾诉这满腹的衷肠，与她互通款曲，私订密约，或是寄给她相思的明镜，用来换取她身上的奇香，仍是不得要领。天公啊，就与我行个方便，让我们在你的眼皮子底下短暂地相会，又有何妨呢？

这阕词当作于词人元祐八年（1093 年）调知溧水后的三年间，是一首描写相思怀人的作品。王明清《挥麈余话》卷二载："周美成为江宁府溧水令，主簿之室，有色而慧，美成每款洽于尊席之间。世所传《风流子》词，盖所寓意焉。……新绿、待月，皆簿厅亭轩之名也。"此说虽未必可信，亦不必拘泥于事实，但这阕词确实抒发的是相思之情。

周邦彦（1056 年—1121 年），字美成，号清真居士，杭州钱塘（今浙江省杭州市）人。北宋文学家、音乐家，婉约派的代表词人之一。

周邦彦自小性格疏散，但勤于读书。宋神宗在位之际，还是太学生的他，就因撰写《汴都赋》歌颂新法，受到皇帝赏识，升任太学正。此后十余年间，却一直在外漂泊，历任庐州教授、溧水县令等职。

宋哲宗亲政后，周邦彦回到开封，任国子监主簿、校书郎等职。宋徽宗时更一度提举大晟府，负责谱制词曲，供奉朝廷，后又外调顺昌府、处州等地。于南京应天府逝世，享年六十六岁，获赠宣奉大夫。

满庭芳·夏日溧水无想山作

周邦彦

风老莺雏，雨肥梅子，午阴嘉树清圆。地卑山近，衣润费炉烟。人静乌鸢yuān自乐，
小桥外、新绿溅溅。凭阑久，黄芦苦竹，拟泛九江船。

年年。如社燕，飘流瀚海，来寄修椽chuán。且莫思身外，长近尊前。憔悴江南倦客，
不堪听、急管繁弦。歌筵yán畔，先安簟diàn枕，容我醉时眠。

Courtyard Full of Fragrance
Write on a Summer Day in Wu Xiang Hill
Zhou Bangyan

In balmy breeze
Fledged orioles in flight,
In gentle rain
The mumes are filling out.
At moon the rounded shadows of the stately trees
Are pools of cool delight.
Low is the plain
With hills about.
The clothes damp need incense smoke to make them dry.
It's so reposeful that e'er crows won't fly.
Beyond the little bridge green water sings its song.
Leaning on rails for long,
I seem to see that exiled poet who
Was fenced in by a tangle of weeds and bamboo.

From year to year
I'm like a swallow swift that leaves
For northern sea and wanders there and here,
But glad to come back under the same old eaves.
Well, why waste thoughts on downs and ups?
Just drink the ever-brimming cups!
For weary southerner with thoughts homebound,
E'en merry flutes and strings would hollow sound.
Beside the banquet table spread
Put mat and pillow on a bed
Where, drunken, I may rest my head!

雏莺在暖风中渐渐长成，梅子受雨水滋润而越长越肥硕，正午的阳光下，绿树亭亭如盖，就连影子也显得清晰圆正。溧水地势低洼靠近山脉，穿在身上的衣服总是湿漉漉的，需要费些炉火来烘干它。幸好这里还算比较安静，没有嘈杂的喧嚣声，就连乌鸦也都自得其乐。小桥外边，新涨的溪水澄澈见底，发出溅溅的水流声。

久久地凭靠着栏杆，放眼望去，遍地都是枯萎的芦苇和清瘦的竹子，此等境遇，跟当年被贬九江、终日泛舟江边的白居易，又有什么区别？

年复一年，我就像社燕一样，终日漂流在瀚海荒漠间，在春社时飞来，到秋社时飞去，只暂时寄身在人家的屋檐下。姑且不再去思虑身外的功名事，不如时常举起手中的酒杯开怀畅饮，一醉解千愁。可我这憔悴的江南倦客，偏生又受不了宴会上激越的丝竹管弦，怕它更添愁绪，奈之若何？最好是在歌筵旁，预先安置好枕席，让我喝醉时便可以就地卧眠，那样的话，烦恼也就不会跟着来了。

宋强焕《片玉词序》：“待制周公，元祐癸酉春中，为邑长于斯。”元祐癸酉，为元祐八年（1093年）。《景定建康志》卷二十溧水县厅壁县令题名：“周邦彦，元祐八年二月到任。何愈，绍圣三年（1096年）三月到任。”则此词当于此三年间作于溧水。

周邦彦在元祐二年（1087年）外放，辗转了七年，才当上了官职卑微的溧水知县，而这对素来具有大抱负的他来说，是一桩十分苦闷的事情。任期内的某个夏日，他游览了溧水境内的无想山，顿时感慨万千，并创作了这阕欲求解脱的抒情词。

解语花·上元

周邦彦

风销绛①jiàng蜡，露浥②yì红莲，花市光相射。桂华流瓦。纤云散，耿耿素娥欲下。

衣裳淡雅。看楚女纤腰一把。箫鼓喧，人影参差，满路飘香麝shè。

因念都城放夜。望千门如昼，嬉笑游冶。钿车罗帕。相逢处，自有暗尘随马。

年光是也。唯只见、旧情衰谢。清漏移，飞盖归来，从舞休歌罢。

①绛蜡一作：焰蜡

②红莲一作：烘炉

Intelligent Flower
Lantern Festival

Zhou Bangyan

The candle flames redden the breeze;
The lotus lanterns seem to freeze.
The sky brightens the fair and the fair the sky.
The tiles are steeped in moonlight
When fleecy clouds disperse in flight,
The Moon Goddess would come down from on high.
In elegant dress appear
The southern maidens tender
With waist so slender.
The drums boom far and near,
The crowd's shadows rise and fall,
Fragrance wafts over all.

I remember the capital's lantern night:
A thousand doors overwhelmed with light,
People made merry in laughter.
From golden cabs silk handkerchiefs dropped down,
The gallants ran after
The cabs as dim dust raised by steeds in the town.
But years have passed
Now I see only for my part
With an unfeeling heart
How time flies fast.
The cabs will not come back again
And people have sung and danced in vain.

通明的烛焰在风中被慢慢销蚀，夜露浸湿了莲花灯，街市上灯火辉煌，交相辉映，又是一年元宵到。

皎洁的月光在屋瓦上流泻，淡淡的云层散去，仿佛光彩照人的嫦娥翩然欲下。这些南方的美女们，个个都细腰如柳，穿着素淡雅致的衣裳，却是掩盖不住她们秀美的容颜、窈窕的身姿。大街小巷上，到处都箫鼓喧腾，人影攒动，满路上都飘散着脂粉的香气，怎一个心动了得。

不由得又想起了当年在京师见过的花灯之夜，千家万户都无一例外地在各自的门前张灯结彩，那璀璨的灯火，迅即便将一整座城池照耀得如同白昼般清朗明丽。整个东京城的百姓几乎倾巢而出，大家结伴游赏在挂满花灯的大街小巷，每个人的脸上都挂着笑容。

香车上不时有女子往车下扔着罗帕，那是因为她们遇见了心仪的男子。乍然相逢，两情相悦，必有血气方刚的风流少年骑着马，暗暗尾随着香车一路同行，所过之处，都是马蹄扬起的尘土。每年的元宵节都是那么热闹非凡，只可惜，历尽沧桑的我，已经无复旧日嬉戏游冶的情怀，更没有心思去学那小儿女的模样惺惺作态。

夜渐渐深了，我再也无心观赏这灯月交辉的景象，亦无意流连于追欢逐爱的风情，就乘着车子赶紧回到了官邸。人啊，纵使高兴到了极致，那狂欢达旦的歌舞也终有了尽的时候，与其灯阑人散，扫兴归来，还不如早点离开热闹的场合，留不尽之余味，一个人默默咀嚼的好。

关于这阕词的具体创作地点和时间，历来就有各种异说。清人周济《宋四家词选》谓是“在荆南作”“当与《齐天乐》同时”；近人陈思《清真居士年谱》则以此词为周邦彦知明州（今浙江省宁波市）时所作，时在宋徽宗政和五年（1115 年）。

木兰花·乙卯吴兴寒食

张先

龙头舴（zé）艋（měng）吴儿竞，笋柱秋千游女并。
芳洲拾翠暮忘归，秀野踏青来不定。
行云去后遥山暝，已放笙歌池院静。
中庭月色正清明，无数杨花过无影。

Magnolia Flowers
Cold Food Day in 1075

Zhang Xian

The Southerners in dragon boats contest in speed,
Fair maidens on the bamboo seat swing to and fro.
Plucking sweet flowers, women linger in the mead,
Treading on the green field, townspeople come and go.

The floating clouds blown off, dim is the distant hill;
Flute songs are hushed, deserted gardens quiet.
Steeped in the moon's pure light, the middle court is still;
Leaving no shadow, countless willow downs run dot.

吴地的儿郎们在江面上赛着形如蚱蜢的小龙舟，游春的姑娘们成双入对地荡着竹竿制成的秋千，一时间，锣鼓喧天，欢声笑语响彻云霄。有人在水边采集百草，直至夜幕降临，依然流连不归，放眼望去，景色秀美的郊野上，踏青的人更是一波接着一波，往来不绝。

结伴出游的姑娘们慢慢散去后，远处的山峦也在暮色中逐渐变得愈加昏暗。歌声戛然而止，小桥流水的庭院里一片清幽岑静，自是心旷神怡。回头望望，万籁俱寂，院中的月色正是清新明亮的时候，遗憾的是，只有无数的柳絮孤独地飘浮在空中，却没有在地上留下一丝倩影。

宋神宗熙宁八年（1075 年），退居故乡的张先，在吴兴度过了他人生中第八十六个寒食节，并写下了这阕清新可爱的词作。朱彝尊《静志居诗话》说："张子野吴兴寒食词'中庭月色正清明，无数杨花过无影'，余尝叹其工绝，世所传'三影'之上。"

张先（990 年—1078 年），字子野，乌程（今浙江省湖州市）人。北宋词人，婉约派代表人物。

酒泉子·长忆观潮

潘阆

长忆观潮，满郭人争江上望。来疑沧海尽成空，万面鼓声中。
弄潮儿向涛头立，手把红旗旗不湿。别来几向梦中看，梦觉尚心寒。

Fountain of Wine

Pan Lang

I still remember watching tidal bore,
The town poured out on river shore.
It seemed the sea had emptied all its water here,
And thousands of drums were beating far and near.

At the crest of huge billows the swimmers did stand,
Yet dry remained red flags they held in hand.
Come back,I saw in dreams the tide o'er flow the river,
Awake,I feel my heart with fear still shiver.

时常想起昔年在钱塘江畔观潮的情景，满城男女老少都争先恐后地挤向江堤，全神贯注地望向那浩浩汤汤的江水，好似这世间再也没有比这更值得关注的事了。

潮水涌来时，让人怀疑远处的大海仿佛在一瞬间被掏空了，那潮声就像一万面齐发的鼓点，乍然敲落在江涛上，声势喧天，震耳欲聋。

踏浪献技的艺人，总是迎着波涛，屹立在江潮上，表演他们的各种拿手好戏，手中举着的红旗却从来都没有被水濡湿过，令人叹为观止。

此去经年，也曾多次在睡梦中梦到当初观潮时的盛况，每每都无一例外地，在梦醒时分仍会觉得惊心动魄，意犹未尽。

潘阆曾以卖药为生，一度流浪到杭州。他亲眼看见过钱塘潮的壮丽宏伟，以至于今后的日子里曾多次梦见涨潮的情形，而这阕词便是他回顾昔日的观潮盛景所作。

潘阆（约962年—1009年），字梦空，一说逍遥，号逍遥子。宋初著名隐士。河北大名（今河北省邯郸市大名县东北）人，一说扬州人。

性格疏狂，曾两次坐事亡命。宋真宗时释其罪，任滁州参军。有诗名，风格与孟郊、贾岛相类，亦工词，今仅存《酒泉子》十首。

沁园春·忆黄山

汪莘

三十六峰，三十六溪，长锁清秋。对孤峰绝顶，云烟竞秀；悬崖峭壁，瀑布争流。洞里桃花，仙家芝草，雪后春正取次游。亲曾见，是龙潭白昼，海涌潮头。

当年黄帝浮丘，有玉枕玉床还在不？向天都月夜，遥闻凤管；翠微霜晓，仰盼龙楼。砂穴长红，丹炉已冷，安得灵方闻早修？谁知此，问源头白鹿，水畔青牛。

Spring in a Pleasure Garden
Yellow Mountains Recalled

Wang Shen

Thirty-six peaks
And thirty-six streams
Have long locked clear autumn in dreams.
In face of lonely peaks and lofty crest,
Clouds and mist vie to look their best.
Over cliffs steep and high
Cascades in roaring vie.
In the cave grow peach flowers,
And life-long herbs in divine bowers.
After spring snow one by one they will come in sight.
I have seen with my eyes
The Dragon's Pool in broad daylight,
The sea in angry billows rise.

Of the Yellow Emperor's reign,
Do the jade bed and pillow still remain?
From the Celestial Town in moonlight,
I've heard the phoenix flute play music bright.
On green mountains in frosty morning hours,
I've looked up to Dragon's towers.
Still red is the elixir old,
But the Magical Stove is cold.
How could a mortal turn divine?
If you do want to know,
Ask the white deer at the source fine
Or the waterside buffalo.

三十六座山峰，三十六条溪流，长年云雾缭绕，清幽如秋，这便是层峦叠嶂、青葱蓊郁的千古名胜黄山。抬头，但见孤峰绝顶之上，云遮烟绕，竞相展现着各自的丰姿，那悬崖峭壁之上，更有无数条争流的瀑布自天而降，好不壮观。

炼丹峰的炼丹洞中，有形似桃花的灵异怪石；轩辕峰下的彩芝源，曾是轩辕黄帝采摘灵芝的地方。正月里，正是春天萌芽的季节，雪过天晴之际，我便来了一次说走就走的黄山之旅，想要去看看那里的桃花石和仙家留下的芝草。

黄山果真是个神奇的地方，我曾在阳光明媚的白昼，亲眼看见过白龙潭壮丽奇谲的景象。若不是亲身经历，很难想象那里的潭水居然会像海潮般汹涌澎湃、波浪翻滚，至今都让人犹疑在梦中。

当年，黄帝和浮丘公都曾游历过黄山，他们用过的玉枕、玉床等卧具，而今都还在吗？凝眸，望向天都峰澄澈的夜空，月色正好，隐约间，却听到了从远处传来的笙箫之声，怎不让人心旷神怡。

拂晓时分的翠微峰，比之夜色笼罩下的天都峰，则显得更加清丽幽静。总是喜欢在晨光微曦、浓霜还未彻底消逝之际，翘首望向遥远的天空，企盼能够见到传说中神秘而又曼妙的海市蜃楼，可这种机会却是可遇而不可求的。

定睛望去，浮丘公当初提炼丹砂的石穴，尽管依旧还是原来的朱红色，经久不衰，但遗憾的是，炼丹炉中的炉火早已熄灭，丹炉也跟着冷却了有数千个年头了，却叹，而今的我，该如何才能得到灵丹仙方，早早地修炼成仙？问苍天，究竟有谁会知道答案呢？看来也只好去问问那源头的白鹿和水畔的青牛了。

词人早年屏居黄山刻苦攻读，曾三次上书朝廷言事，每一次都石沉大海，未能引起执政者的关注与重视。晚年筑室于柳溪，自号方壶居士，对故乡山水有着极其深厚的感情，他不仅作词吟咏黄山，还在书房里挂满了黄山的图卷，“向画里嬉游卧里看”，自觉“此身真在黄山中也”，便是词人在游览黄山时所写。

汪莘（1155 年—1227 年），南宋诗人。字叔耕，号柳塘，徽州休宁（今属安徽）人，终身布衣，与朱熹友善。

隐居黄山，研究《周易》，旁及释、老。宋宁宗嘉定年间，曾三次上书朝廷，陈述天变、人事、民穷、吏污等弊病，以及行师布阵的方法，却都没有得到朝廷的答复。徐谊知建康时，想把他作为遁世隐士推荐给朝廷，但最终也没能成功。

南浦·春水

王沂孙

柳下碧粼粼，认麹(qū)尘乍生，色嫩如染。清溜满银塘，东风细，参差縠(hú)纹初遍。

别君南浦，翠眉曾照波痕浅。再来涨绿迷旧处，添却残红几片。

蒲萄过雨新痕，正拍拍轻鸥，翩翩小燕。帘影蘸楼阴，芳流去，应有泪珠千点。

沧浪一舸，断魂重唱蘋(pín)花怨。采香幽泾鸳鸯睡，谁道湔(jiān)裙人远。

The Southern Riverside Spring Water

Wang Yisun

Green water shimmers under willow trees;
Dustlike things grow by riverside
With tender hue as if they were dyed.
The silver pond of clear drops full,
The gentle eastern breeze
Spreads ripples here and there on the pool.
We bade adieu on Southern shore;
Your eyebrows mirrored have left on the waves your trace.
Green waves rise when you come again to the old place:
You'll find a few fallen petals more.

On grape-hued water you'll find new traces of rain,
The gulls flap their wings light
With young swallows in flight.
In the shade of the tower your screen appears
With your fragrance out of sight,
You may find thousands of drops of tears.
A lonely boat on the main,
You'd hear the heart-broken song of duckweed again.
The lovebirds sleep on the fragrant pathway.
Who knows the rosy dress is far away?

柳树下碧绿的江水，端的是波光粼粼，清澈见底。定睛望去，忽地发现柳枝上刚刚绽出了细小的新芽，新嫩的色泽，如同被染过一般清丽明艳。

澄澈的春水填满了江塘，当和煦的东风轻轻拂来之际，整个水面都泛起了潋滟的波纹，层层叠叠地，布满她的眼帘。一切的一切，都让她又想起在南浦和他分别时的情景，青黛色的眉影，曾映照在那一池浅浅的春水里，自是美得无以复加，更让他心生无限怜爱。

遗憾的是，当她再度来临的时候，南浦的水位早已漫过了他们曾经话别的地方，而那渺渺无垠的水面上，却又无端地多出了几片凋零的红花，怎不惹人惆怅莫名？

碧绿的江水，在经过雨水的洗礼之后，闪耀着葡萄酒一样新亮的色泽。鸥鸟在水面上轻轻拍打着翅膀，乳燕翩跹着在半空中翱翔，好一派祥和宁谧的景象。珠帘和楼台的倒影，仿若浸蘸在这一池春水中，让人心生无限遐想。只是，这潋滟的波光里，应该还裹挟着痴心女子的千点相思泪珠，正随着起伏不定的浪花轻轻地流去，却又不知道它们究竟会流向何处。

他乘舟离去之后，浩浩的浪涛之间，便只留下她一个人，裹着满心的失落，失魂落魄地频频唱起那首断肠的《蘋花怨》。采蘋的幽径间，时常可以看到鸳鸯成双成对地栖息在一处，可那远去的人儿，何时才能想起她这闺中的思妇呢？

这阕词题为“春水”，乃咏“春水”之作，但妙就妙在全词居然没有一个字提到春水，却又句句都是在写春水，足见词人文字功力之深。王沂孙是一个特别善于状物的词人，在他的笔下，无论梅花、春水、柳或落叶，都给人以清新别致的感受，而这阕词中，他不仅直接为春水涂色，回忆之际也处处充斥着春水画境，且有着浓烈的生活情致。

王沂孙（约1230年—约1290年），字圣与，又字咏道，号碧山，又号中仙，因家住玉笥山，故又号玉笥山人。会稽（今浙江省绍兴市）人，曾任庆元路（今宁波市鄞州区）学正。南宋词人。

王沂孙工词，风格类同周邦彦，含蓄深婉，如《花犯·苔梅》之类，而其清峭处，又颇似姜夔，所以张炎说他“琢语峭拔，有（姜）白石意度”。尤以咏物为工，如《齐天乐·蝉》《水龙吟·白莲》等，皆善于体会物象以寄托感慨。其词章法缜密，在宋末格律派词人中，是一位有着显著艺术个性的词家，与周密、张炎、蒋捷，并称为“宋末词坛四大家”。

第二章

红笺×无色

CHAPTER TWO

On rosy papers and they fade

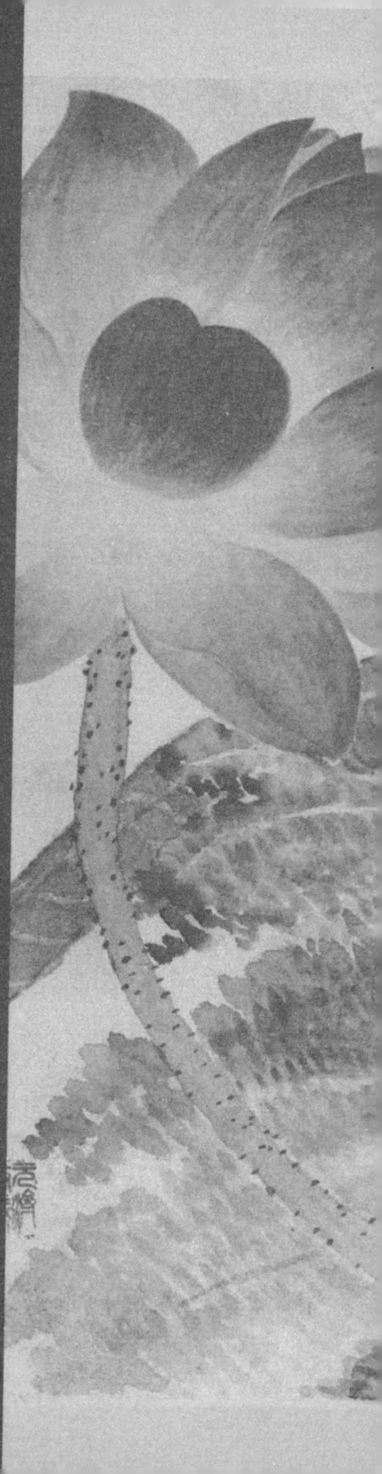

眉妩·新月

王沂孙

渐新痕悬柳，淡彩穿花，依约破初暝。便有团圆意，深深拜，相逢谁在香径。画眉未稳，料素娥、犹带离恨。最堪爱、一曲银钩小，宝帘挂秋冷。千古盈亏休问。叹慢磨玉斧，难补金镜。太液池犹在，凄凉处、何人重赋清景。故山夜永。试待他、窥户端正。看云外山河，还老尽、桂花影。

Lovely Eyebrows
The Crescent Moon

Wang Yisun

Gradually the new moon hangs on the willow tree
And' mid the flowers sheds pale beams
As if day broke the twilight dreams.
The crescent would turn round with glee.
To it I bow.
Whom should I meet on fragrant pathway now?
It's like the Moon Goddess' undulating brow,
Gnawed by her parting sorrow still.
What's loveliest of all,
A hooklike silver crescent small
Hangs on the pearly curtain of Autumn's chill.

From age to age it waxes and wanes.
Don't ask how long!
Though you may whet the axe of jade,
How can you mend the mirror of gold?
The royal garden still remains,
But now so drear. Who'll sing a song
In praise of marble balustrade?
In native land the night is endless as of old.
I'll wait until
The moon turns round and peeps into my room.
O see beyond the clouds the hill and rill,
Where even laurel trees grow old and cast a gloom!

一轮新月，仿佛一弯眉痕，缓缓挂上了柳梢。素淡的月彩，悄悄穿透花枝，像往常一样，依约将初降的暮色划破。温婉的月色，冷不防让人顿生团圆的意愿，那闺中的佳人，更是弯下腰，对着月亮的方向深深地拜了又拜，祈盼能够与心上的人儿，相逢在那花香迷人的小径上。

这新月，看上去就像美人的秀眉没有画好似的，料想一定是嫦娥还带着满腹的离情别绪。最令人喜爱的是，那弯新月恰似宝帘上的银钩，就那么挂在澄澈明净的天空上，小巧而玲珑，美得出尘又娴静。

自古以来，月亮就有圆亏缺盈，不必细问究竟。叹只叹，吴刚徒然把玉斧磨快，也难以将此轮残月补全。故都的太液池依然还在，只是这一片凄清冷寂里，又有谁人能够重新描画出昔日的清丽湖山呢？

故乡的深夜，漫长而悠远，只盼着月亮快些圆满澄明，端端正正地照耀我的门庭。遗憾的是，月影中的山河依旧广阔无垠，而我却已经默默老去，以后的以后，也只能在桂花月影中看到故国山河的壮丽与繁华了。

唐人有拜新月之俗，宋人也有新月下置宴饮酒之举，而临宴题咏新月，乃是南宋文士的风雅习尚。这阕词写于南宋覆亡之后，其时新月依旧，习俗相仍，然而江山却已易主，故每于人月相对之时，自然便勾起了词人的兴亡之痛。面对宗祖沉沦，今昔巨变之痛，词人创作此词，借咏新月寄寓了对亡国的哀思。

贺圣朝·留别

叶清臣

满斟绿醑（xǔ）留君住。莫匆匆归去。三分春色二分愁，更一分风雨。

花开花谢、都来几许。且高歌休诉。不知来岁牡丹时，再相逢何处。

Homage to the Imperial Court
Detain the Parting

Ye Qingchen

With cups full of green wine, I ask you to stay:
Don't go so soon away!
Two-thirds of spring are full of grief and pain,
One-third of wind and rain.

The flowers blow and fade.
How many have stayed?
Let's chant aloud! Of what can we complain?
Next year when peonies blow in vain,
Where can we meet again?

斟满淡绿色的美酒，请君再留下多住上几日，不要就这样匆匆地离去。剩下的三分春色，二分都是离愁别绪，一分又充满了凄风苦雨，你怎么舍得丢下我一个人，就这么走了呢？

年年都可以见到花开花谢，从来都没有间断过，那相思之情又有多少呢？现在，就让我们举杯畅饮，高歌一曲，不要再谈论任何伤感的事情，只把眼下的快乐进行到底，好吗？今朝有酒今朝醉，明年牡丹盛开的时候，还不知道我们又会在哪里相逢呢！

这阕词是酒席筵前留别之作，词人满斟美酒，劝友人尽情享受眼前的欢乐。全词精心铺叙，情意殷切，既表现出了词人伤春惜别的情怀，也流露出了人生萍寄之感。

叶清臣（1000年—1049年），字道卿，长洲（今江苏省苏州市）人，一作乌程（今浙江省湖州市）人。北宋名臣。

因论范仲淹、余靖以言事被黜事，为宋仁宗采纳，范仲淹等人得以近徙。知永兴军时，修复三白渠，溉田六千顷，政绩显著，后人称颂。著作今存《述煮茶小品》等，《全宋词》录其词一首。

忆故人·烛影摇红

王诜

烛影摇红，向夜阑，乍酒醒、心情懒。
尊前谁为唱《阳关》，离恨天涯远。
无奈云沉雨散。凭阑干、东风泪眼。
海棠开后，燕子来时，黄昏庭院。

Old Friends Recalled

Wang Shen

The candle flickers red
At dead of night,
I wake from wine in bed,
My mind in idle plight.
Who sings before a cup of wine songs of goodbye?
My parting grief goes as far as the sky.

What can I do after you brought fresh shower
For my thirsting flower?
I lean on balustrade,
In eastern breeze my eyes shed tears.
When the crabapple flowers fade,
The swallow disappears,
The evening is hard in my courtyard.

夜深人静，刚刚从沉醉中醒来的我，独自对着摇曳的烛光，自是心灰意懒，黯然神伤。冷不防，突地想起昨晚在送别的酒筵上，我为他唱起的那曲《阳关三叠》。而今，他已离我远去，再也无法看到他眉梢眼角的清欢，那么，就让我这满腔的离愁别恨，永远都跟随着他直到天涯海角吧！

却无奈，往日的欢声笑语，转眼之间，便即烟消云散，怎不让人唏嘘叹息？晨起懒梳妆，只凭栏远眺，却是依旧不见他的踪影，一阵东风倏忽吹来，不由得悲从中来，泪如泉涌。就这样痴痴凝望着远方，不知不觉间，已近黄昏，海棠花默默地凋谢，燕子正归巢，落日之下的庭院，则显得更加凄清冷寂了。

这阕《忆故人》的词意，与调名相仿，为代言体形式，写的是一个痴情女子对故人的忆念，全词深情缱绻，感人至深。

宋词应歌而作，而歌者多为女性，为使演唱达到生动逼真的效果，所以词人往往会在词作中以女性的视角，去写景、状物、抒情。这阕词便是词人王诜从一个女子的角度，去写对故人的忆念。

王诜（1048 年—1104 年），字晋卿，太原（今山西省太原市）人，后迁汴京（今河南省开封市），北宋画家。

北宋熙宁二年（1069 年），娶宋英宗之女蜀国大长公主，拜左卫将军、驸马都尉。元丰二年（1079 年），因受苏轼牵连贬官均州。元祐元年（1086 年）复登州刺史、驸马都尉。卒谥荣安。

王诜擅画山水，学王维、李成，喜作烟江云山、寒林幽谷，水墨清润明洁，青绿设色高古绝俗。亦能书，善属文，其词语言清丽，情致缠绵，音调谐美。存世作品有《渔村小雪图》《烟江叠嶂图》《溪山秋霁图》等。

鹊桥仙·七夕

苏轼

缑gōu山仙子，高情云渺，不学痴牛𫘤ái女。凤箫声断月明中，举手谢、时人欲去。

客槎曾犯，银河波浪，尚带天风海雨。相逢一醉是前缘，风雨散、飘然何处？

Immortal at the Magpie Bridge
Farewell on Double Seventh Eve

Su Shi

Like the immortal leaving the crowd,
Wafting above the cloud,
Unlike the Cowherd and the Maid who fond remain,
You blow your flute in moonlight,
Waving your hand, you go in flight.

Your boat will go away
Across the Milky Way,
In celestial wind and rain.
We've met and drunk as if by fate.
Where will you waft when wind and rain abate?

居住在缑山上的仙人王子乔，性格清高，懒得学那贪恋红尘的牛郎织女，要下凡到尘世间走上一遭。那一年，在皎洁的月光下，他放下嘴边吹奏的凤箫，挥一挥手，便即告别人间，飞仙而去，从此后，更鲜少有人看到过他的踪迹。

听说黄河上的竹筏能够直上银河，一路上还挟带着天风海雨，而今，我们也一起泛舟而行，是不是也能像王子乔一样羽化登仙呢？相逢一醉，是前生的缘分，然分别之际，谁又能知道，今后的我们会各自飘零向何方呢？

宋神宗熙宁七年（1074年），苏轼和好友陈令举乘舟游玩，一边饮酒，一边欢快地畅谈。然而，相聚之后总是要分别的，为表达自己对陈令举的依依不舍，词人便写下这阕词送给他。

全词不仅摆脱了描摹儿女情态的俗套之法，在格调上，更用飘逸超旷取代了缠绵悱恻之风，读来深感词人的超凡脱俗以及卓尔不群的姿态。

苏轼（1037年—1101年），字子瞻，一字和仲，号铁冠道人、东坡居士，世称苏东坡、苏仙、坡仙。眉州眉山（今四川省眉山市）人，祖籍河北栾城（今河北省石家庄市栾城区）。北宋著名文学家、书法家、美食家、画家。

鹊桥仙·富沙七夕为友人赋

赵以夫

翠绡xiāo心事，红楼欢宴，深夜沉沉无暑。竹边荷外再相逢，又还是、浮云飞去。

锦笺尚湿，珠香未歇，空惹闲愁千缕。寻思不似鹊桥人，犹自得、一年一度。

Immortal at the Magpie Bridge
Written for a Friend on the Double Seventh Eve

Zhao Yifu

The green-dress songstress told me what she'd say,
When first we feasted in the bower red,
The night was deep, so cool and clear.
Beyond bamboos and lotus blooms we met again,
Again like floating cloud she flew away.

Her letter is still wet,
Perfume not dispersed yet.
I feel in vain
Sorrow in thread.
Unlike the cowherd and his sweet
Who could still meet
Once every year.

天凉暑退，夜色沉沉，七夕欢快的宴席上，在画梁雕栋的红楼里，她满面娇羞地偷偷赠给他一条碧绿色的丝巾，一往情深的心事，早就毫无保留地，写在了她那一双水汪汪的大眼睛里。

荷塘附近的竹林边，是一个美丽僻静的所在，也是他们瞒着别人再度幽会的地方。他们一边呼吸着新鲜的空气，一边透过十里荷风，说着无尽的相思，遗憾的是，这次短暂的聚首很快就过去了，仓促得仿佛空中飘浮的云彩，刹那间便即消逝得无影无踪，一去不复返。

终于按捺不住满腹的相思之痛，提笔给他写下一封长长的书信，想要一诉衷肠，却不料，那悲伤的泪珠，竟又不自觉地滴落了下来，瞬间便打湿了手边精致华美的信笺。小楼中仍然弥漫着他的气息，只可惜，往事恰如云烟，每想念他一次，便会徒增一次烦恼，只添了千丝万缕的愁绪。暗思忖，牛郎织女终年都被银河阻隔在两地，尚能在每年的七夕之夜鹊桥相会，可自己却与他再无相见之日，念及于此，便又心痛莫名，珠泪暗垂。

词人任职福建富沙之时，逢七夕之夜，与友人同僚共聚良宵。席间，词人听友人讲述了一位歌伎的情史，闻后感慨不已，遂赋得此词。赵以夫从歌姬的视角出发，将牛郎织女与歌姬的不同遭遇相比照，加深了歌姬的不幸，同时也表达了词人对歌姬的同情，以及对那些玩弄他人感情的纨绔子弟的深恶痛绝。

赵以夫(1189年—1256年)，字用父，号虚斋，福州府长乐县(今福建省福州市长乐区)人。南宋嘉定十年(1217年)进士，历知邵武军、漳州，皆有治绩。嘉熙初年(1237年)，任枢密都承旨兼国史院编修官，二年，知庆元府兼沿海制置副使，四年，复除枢密都承旨；淳祐五年(1245年)出知建康府，七年，知平江府。以资政殿学士致仕。著有《虚斋乐府》。

一丛花令·伤高怀远几时穷

张先

伤高怀远几时穷？无物似情浓。离愁正引千丝乱，更东陌、飞絮蒙蒙。嘶sī骑渐遥，征尘不断，何处认郎踪。

双鸳池沼水溶溶，南北小桡ráo通。梯横画阁黄昏后，又还是、斜月帘栊。沉恨细思，不如桃杏，犹解嫁东风。

Song of Flower Shrub

Zhang Xian

When will the sorrow end
To watch my parting friend
From a tower above?
Nothing is so intense as love.
My sorrow interweaves
A thousand twigs of willow leaves;
The pathway east of the town
Is shrouded in wafting willow down.
His neighing steed is far away,
A cloud of dust still darkening the day.
Where is the place
To find my lover's trace?

A pair of lovebirds seems to melt in water clean:
Little leaflike boats go
North and south, to and fro.
After dusk in the twilight
I dare not go up the painted bower on the height.
What will again be seen
But the waning moon shining on window-screen?
How deeply I envy peach and apricot trees
Newly wed to and oft caressed by vernal breeze!

一次次登高望远，一遍遍苦苦思念着远方的人儿，这满腹的忧伤，到底什么时候才能有个终结？再也没有任何事物，比感情更为浓烈，也没有任何感情，能够比得过我对你的思念。

离愁别绪，正牵连着千丝万缕的柳条，在眼前辗转纷飞，更何况东陌之上，飘飞的柳絮早就遮满了天空，怎不惹人伤心难禁？当日，你骑着嘶鸣着的马儿离我远去，慢慢消逝在飞扬的尘土之中，而今烟水茫茫，又叫我到哪里去寻找你的踪迹呢？

放眼望去，远处的池塘里，波光粼粼，一对鸳鸯正在欢快地戏水，时不时地还能看到划着桨的小舟往来于池水的北岸和南岸。黄昏过后，雕梁画栋的楼阁上，通往楼下的梯子已经撤去，唯有一弯斜月，依旧低低地照着窗扉和珠帘，怎一个寂寞了得。

怀着深深的怨恨，我反复思量，为什么我的命运竟然还比不过桃花杏花，就连它们都可以如愿以偿地嫁给东风，而我却还要在这里左顾右盼，没个头绪？

这阕词描写了一位女子在她的恋人离开之后，独处深闺之际的无限相思与无尽愁恨。张先的众多艳词，大多感情浅薄，而此词却情真意切，别具一格，无论从思想性还是艺术性来看，都颇为值得称道。

减字木兰花·春情

王安国

画桥流水，雨湿落红飞不起。月破黄昏，帘里余香马上闻。

徘徊不语，今夜梦魂何处去。不似垂杨，犹解飞花入洞房。

Shortened Form of Magnolia Flower
Spring Love

Wang Anguo

Beneath the painted bridge water flows by;
No fallen flowers wet with rain can ever fly.
At dusk the moon is seen;
On horse I still smell the fragrance behind the screen.

Silently lingering around,
Where will my dreaming soul tonight be found?
Unlike the weeping willow,
Whose down will fly into her room and on her pillow.

饰有花纹图案的小桥下，流水潺潺，波光潋滟，好一个清幽僻静的所在。落花被雨水淋湿，沾在地上，再也无法随风起舞。月光缓缓穿破黄昏的晦暗，那藏身帘内的佳人，她身上散发出的脂粉余香，我坐在马上依旧能够清晰地闻到。

下得马来，独自徘徊在房前屋后，却不知道，今夜里，我的魂儿将要随梦追逐她到什么地方去。小娘子啊，你怎么还比不上垂杨那般多情？垂杨还懂得让花絮飞入幽深的居室，你又怎生舍得一直让我踯躅在门外呢？

但凡以“春情”为题的词作，大抵都是写闺中女子当春怀人的思绪，而王安国这阕小令却另辟蹊径，写了一个男子在暮春时节，对一位女子思而不见、爱而不得的愁情，内容与贺铸的《青玉案》相仿。贺作另有寄托，此词有无别的寓意尚难确定。

王安国（1028年—1074年），字平甫，王安石大弟。抚州临川（今江西省抚州市）人，北宋著名诗人。他器识磊落，文思敏捷，曾巩谓其“于书无所不通，其明于是非得失之理为尤详，其文闳富典重，其诗博而深”。

卜算子·答施

乐婉

相思似海深，旧事如天远。泪滴千千万万行，更使人、愁肠断。

要见无因见，拚了终难拚。若是前生未有缘，待重结、来生愿。

Song of Divination
In Reply to Her Love

Le Wan

My love is deep as the sea high;
The past is far away as the sky.
The thousand streams of tears I shed
Make me heart-broken and half dead.

If I cannot see you again,
Why don't we cut to kill my pain?
If we are fated not to be man and wife,
Let us be married in another life!

自与你离别之后，痛苦的相思便如沧海一样深而无际，让我备受煎熬。昔日的欢好，那点点滴滴的忆念，到如今，就像辽阔的天幕一样，距离我有千里万里之遥，再也无法触及。为你，我流尽了千行万行的泪水，却又无一例外地，愁断了肠，痛断了肝。

想要与你相见，却又找不到相见的理由；想要结束这段感情，却又始终舍弃不了。你我若是前生没有缘分，那么就等待来生，再结为举案齐眉、白首偕老的夫妻吧！

南宋名妓乐婉，与施酒监情投意合。施酒监在京任职期满，即将调往他处，却无力给乐婉赎身。施酒监临行前写了一阕《卜算子》词送给乐婉："相逢情便深，恨不相逢早。识尽千千万万人，终不如伊好。别尔登长道，转觉添烦恼。楼外朱楼独倚阑，满目围芳草。"乐婉读了这阕词后心如刀绞，便强忍住悲痛，提笔写下了这阕《卜算子·答施》，以示与情人诀别。

乐婉（生卒年不详），宋代杭州名妓，为施酒监所悦。施酒监曾有词相赠别，乐婉和之，即今传世的《卜算子·答施》，收录于《花草粹编》卷二，引自南宋杨湜《古今词话》（已佚）。

第三章

雨荷×烟柳

CHAPTER THREE

Lotus in rain and mist-veiled willow green

洞仙歌·咏柳

苏轼

江南腊尽，早梅花开后，分付新春与垂柳。细腰肢自有入格风流，仍更是、骨体清英雅秀。

永丰坊那畔，尽日无人，谁见金丝弄晴昼？断肠是飞絮时，绿叶成阴，无个事、一成消瘦。又莫是东风逐君来，便吹散眉间一点春皱。

Song of a Fairy in the Cave

Su Shi

By the end of the year on the Southern shore
When early mume blossoms disappear,
The newcome spring dwells on the weeping willow tree,
Its slender waist reveals a personality free,
And what is more,
Its trunk appears more elegant and free.

Along the way
There is no sight-seer all the day.
Who'd come to see your golden thread in sunlight sway?
Your heart would break to see catkins fly,
Your green leaves make a shade of deep dye.
Having nothing to do,
You would grow thinner, too.
If you come again with vernal breeze now,
It would dispel the vernal grief on your brow.

腊月的尽头，江南的早梅花绽放过后，整个世界便都要分付给又一个新春，还有眼前这飘飞的垂柳。

婀娜多姿的柳树，因为天生生就一副细腰肢，自是窈窕风流，格调高雅，无论经历了多少岁月变迁，依旧还是那么骨骼清奇、秀丽多姿。

永丰坊那边多柳，却是一整天都看不到几个行人，更没有人会注意到它们在明媚的阳光下披拂摇缀的柔丝。

最令人伤神的就是柳絮纷飞的暮春时节，尽管披上了浓密的树荫，枝叶繁茂，却因为终日无所事事，倒又显得愈发地清瘦了。不知道它到底因为什么伤春，也没有办法抚去它内心的惆怅，恐怕也只有追逐着它一起来到春天的东风，才可以一点一点地吹散它紧蹙的眉头，让它变得高兴起来吧！

这阕词的写作年代不可确考，朱祖谋认为词意与《殢人娇》略同，并把它编入宋神宗熙宁十年（1077年）作。据《纪年录》记载，这年的三月一日，苏轼在汴京与王诜会于四照亭，因王诜的侍女倩奴求曲，遂作《洞仙歌》《殢人娇》予之。《殢人娇》题“王都尉席上赠侍人”，与《纪年录》所记相合，其词结句，“须信道、司空自来见惯”，对王诜似有规讽。

据史载，王诜为人“不修细行”，生活作风糜烂，则可见他对歌女侍妾必然都轻薄寡情，那么，倩奴在王诜家中的悲苦遭遇也就可想而知了。《洞仙歌》倘若真是写给倩奴的，其内容当与倩奴有关，词题“咏柳”，实则借柳喻人。

浣溪沙·咏橘

苏轼

菊暗荷枯一夜霜。新苞绿叶照林光。竹篱茅舍出青黄。

香雾噀(xùn)人惊半破，清泉流齿怯初尝。吴姬三日手犹香。

Silk-washing Stream

Su Shi

Chrysanthemums are darkened and lotus flowers lost.
The wood is brightened by leaves green and buds new,
The thatched cot and fence would grow yellow and blue.

Her mouth half open, she smells the fragrance sweet;
She's timid to drink the fountain her teeth meet.
Her hand still fragrant stays for three long days.

一夜霜冻过后，菊花凋残，荷花枯萎，只有橘树不畏严寒，焕发出不一样的风姿。枝头的新橘与翠绿的叶片交相辉映，在阳光的衬托下显得格外惹眼。竹篱笆，茅草屋，都掩映在这一树树青色中泛着金黄的橘林间，为这个萧瑟的秋天增添了几许温暖的色彩。

刚刚剥开手中的橘子，一股甜腻的清香便随同喷洒出的汁液扑面而来，让人惊喜不已。带着几分怯意，第一次品尝橘子，那甜中带酸的汁水在唇齿间如清泉流过，自是回味无穷。据说，江南的女子，只因为剥过橘子，手上的余香都会经三日而不绝。

这阕《浣溪沙》词作于宋神宗元丰五年（1082年）十二月，其时苏轼被贬黄州，生活颇为不顺。黄州盛产橘子，味道醇美，给了苏轼很多灵感，这阕《浣溪沙》，更是以橘子自况，短短几句话，便让一个独立自强、品质高洁的东坡形象，轻松跃然于纸上。

品令·茶词

黄庭坚

凤舞团团饼。恨分破、教孤令。金渠（qú）体净，只轮慢碾，玉尘光莹。汤响松风，早减了、二分酒病。

味浓香永。醉乡路、成佳境。恰如灯下，故人万里，归来对影。口不能言，心下快活自省。

Song of Enjoyment
The Tea

Huang Tingjian

A phoenix dances on the round tea cake
I can't but break,
And lonely feel.
You're clean in golden light,
Ground slowly by a wheel
Into fine powder still jade-bright.
When boiled, you sing like the breeze through the pine.
I feel no longer sick of wine.

Your floral taste will longer stay.
When drunk,
In better state I'm sunk,
Just as by candlelight
A friend comes from far, far away.
We sit face to face, left and right,
Without a word,
Our joy at heart can still be heard.

几只栩栩如生的凤凰，在凤饼茶上团团飞舞。只恨喝茶的时候，要把茶饼掰开，凤凰的图案也随之各分东西，显得既孤单又冷寂。

将茶饼用洁净的金渠慢慢碾成琼粉玉屑后，但见茶末成色纯净，清亮晶莹，端的是茶中极品。加入上好的泉水煎之，汤沸声如风过松林，不知不觉间，已将想要醉酒的意思迅速减退了几分。

煎好的茶水味道醇厚，香气持久。其实，品茶亦能使人醉，但不仅无醉酒之苦，饮后反倒觉得神清气爽，渐入佳境。能喝到这种极品的贡茶是种什么感受呢？这就好比一个人独对一盏孤灯之际，有故人恰好从万里之外赶来相会，此种妙处只可意会不可言传，唯有品茶者才能真正体会到其中的情味。

有宋一代，有尚茶、爱茶的风气，此词写的便是龙凤团茶中的凤饼茶。龙凤团茶极其名贵，是宋代御贡的名品，也是茶中之尊，名冠天下。

黄庭坚生长于茶乡修水，从小就对种茶、采茶、卖茶的生活耳濡目染，所以对茶和茶农都怀有深厚的感情。黄庭坚一生辗转浮沉，四处漂泊，与家乡渐行渐远，但始终蕴染着茶的气息。这阕词把凤饼茶的精良品质，以及人们饮用后的感受，都表达得十分具象，用字巧妙贴切，耐人寻味。

黄庭坚（1045 年—1105 年），字鲁直，乳名绳权，号清风阁、山谷道人、山谷老人、涪翁、涪皤、摩围老人、黔安居士、八桂老人。世称黄山谷、黄太史、黄文节、豫章先生。

洪州分宁（今江西省九江市修水县）人，祖籍浙江金华。北宋著名文学家、书法家、江西诗派开山之祖，也是《二十四孝》中“涤亲溺器”故事的主角。

花犯·小石梅花

周邦彦

粉墙低，梅花照眼，依然旧风味。露痕轻缀。疑净洗铅华，无限佳丽。去年胜赏曾孤倚。冰盘同燕喜。更可惜，雪中高树，香篝gōu熏素被。

今年对花最匆匆，相逢似有恨，依依愁悴。吟望久，青苔上、旋看飞坠。相将见、脆丸荐酒，人正在、空江烟浪里。但梦想、一枝潇洒，黄昏斜照水。

Invaded by Flowers
To Mume Blossoms
Zhou Bangyan

Over low rosy wall appear
The mume flowers, dazzling the eyes
Still as last year.
Lightly adorned with dew, you rise
Like a beauty of the day,
With powder washed away.
Last year I leaned alone on your tree,
And drank and ate from the plate ice-bright.
It is lovely to see
Snow-covered mume carefree
Like a perfuming stove under coverlet white.

In face of your flower this year, I feel time is fleet.
You seem to be grieved when we meet,
Looking still so languid and sweet.
For long I croon,
And see you fall down on green mosses soon.
I would like to eat your fruit fine
While drinking wine.
I seem to be
In mist and on waves free,
But still I dream
Of your detached branch over the evening stream.

粉白的矮墙边，一树梅花闪耀得炫人眼目，那凛冽的暗香、招展的风姿，依旧还是去年的模样。轻盈的花瓣上，缀满了晶莹剔透的露珠，恰似洗去脂粉的美人儿，清新淡雅得让人心旌摇荡，自是风光无限。

记得去年的这个时候，也曾来到此处，独自倚在树边，将它尽情看了个透。明月如同冰盘挂在天边，却有幸与之共赏梅花同欢宴，怎一个逍遥了得。雪中的景致更让人觉得可爱，那被白雪覆盖的高高的梅树，就像熏笼上盖上了一床白色的被子，煞是惊艳。

今年赏花最是匆忙，乍然相逢，心里却有着无尽的悲伤，无论是梅花还是人，看上去，都是一样的憔悴，一样的愁肠百结。久久地屹立在梅花前怅望沉吟，却看见缤纷的落花，打着旋儿，悠悠地飘落到脚边的青苔上，好不凄惶。

将来要有机会再相见，也应该是在青翠的梅子被端上酒宴的季节了。只是那时候，我恐怕又要在浩如烟海的江面上与风浪为伍，更与它渐行渐远，所以便只能将一切神往都寄托于梦想，但愿此身化作梅花一枝，每当夕阳西下之际，就安然地立在水边，静看一世潇洒。

这阕《花犯》咏梅词，当写于周邦彦十年州县宦游生涯期间，较大的可能是写于宋哲宗绍圣三年（1096 年）二月，知溧水县任满、奉调进京之时。

这阕词最大的特点，是在咏梅的时候加入了个人身世之感，用前后盘旋、左顾右盼、姿态横生的手法，多方位、多角度地彰显出自己的个人情感。宋代黄升在《唐宋诸贤绝妙词选》中云："此只咏梅花，而纡徐反复，道尽三年间事，圆美流转如弹丸。"

水龙吟·梨花

周邦彦

素肌应怯余寒，艳阳占立青芜wú地。樊川照日，灵关遮路，残红敛避。传火楼台，妒花风雨，长门深闭。亚帘栊半湿，一枝在手，偏勾引、黄昏泪。

别有风前月底。布繁英、满园歌吹。朱铅退尽，潘妃却酒，昭君乍起。雪浪翻空，粉裳缟gǎo夜，不成春意。恨玉容不见，琼英谩好，与何人比。

Water Dragon Chant
To Pear Blossoms

Zhou Bangyan

To your white skin the lingering cold may do harm;
You stand on your green grass under the sun.
You shine on northern land and cover southern way,
You whom remnant reds would shun.
On Cold Food Day
The wind and rain would envy you,
The Long Gate closed anew.
The low-hanging window curtain half wet appears.
When you stretch a branch out as an arm,
The evening is moved to tears.

In breeze or moonlight quiet
Your blooms run riot.
When songs fulfill your garden place,
Unpowdered and unrouged is your face
Like the beauty before she drinks wine
Or the princess rising like sunshine.
In the air surge the waves snow-white,
Silken dress brightens the night.
Unequalled by other vernal flowers in tears,
When your jade-like face disappears.
Other flowers may be fair,
But with you none can compare.

枝头素白的梨花，应该还在担心上个季节尚未退去的余寒，总是在艳阳高照的时候，尽情舒展着腰肢，娉婷袅娜地屹立在萋萋的芳草地上。

樊川也好，灵关也好，放眼望去，到处都是遮天蔽日、雪白一片的梨花，那些残留在枝头的百花，都因为它的到来，纷纷退避三舍，收敛而去，整个世界都陷入了茫茫的白色之中。

清明时节，端的是斜风细雨，没个停歇，好似它们也都是因为嫉妒梨花，才悄然出现在人间。寂寞深院，长门紧闭，被风吹雨打濡湿的梨花，斜斜地压在户帘和窗牖上，更显妩媚娇艳。轻轻折下一枝在手，偏生又勾引出无限的黄昏泪。

更有唐明皇李隆基和杨贵妃一起在梨园演绎的那些风流韵事，给梨花又增添了一层迷幻的色彩。想当年，每到暮春时节，梨园里梨花胜雪，丝竹声、歌声、欢笑声，此起彼伏，是何等的让人叹为观止。

这纯洁无瑕的梨花，像极了褪去胭脂铅粉的女子，美得无以复加，也只有醉酒后的潘妃和冰清玉洁的王昭君，才能与之媲美。梨花之好，即便是连雪花和翻滚中的白色浪涛都难以与之匹敌，而能够在黑夜中照亮天空的李花，也不及它万分之一的春意浓。

恨只恨，而今空有一树繁盛的梨花，却再也无法见到杨玉环那样的绝世佳人了，即便它开得再俏丽再冶艳，又能跟谁比美呢？

这阕词用拟人的写法，极其生动地写出梨花之美，以洁白的肌肤比喻梨花的清新素雅，更是别出心裁。词中大量引用典故，让梨花更具人文气息与历史魅力，有《离骚》初服之意。

六丑·蔷薇谢后作

周邦彦

正单衣试酒，怅客里、光阴虚掷。愿春暂留，春归如过翼，一去无迹。为问花何在，[1]夜来风雨，葬楚宫倾国。钗钿堕处遗香泽。乱点桃蹊，轻翻柳陌。多情为谁追惜。但蜂媒蝶使，时叩窗隔。

东园岑寂。渐蒙笼暗碧。静绕珍丛底，成叹息。长条故惹行客，似牵衣待话，别情无极。残英小、强簪巾帻(zé)。终不似、一朵钗头颤袅，向人欹侧。漂流处、莫趁潮汐。恐断红、尚有相思字，何由见得。

①花何在一作：家何在

Six Toughies
Faded Roses

Zhou Bangyan

Again it's time to taste new wine in dresses light.
How I regret to have misspent my time day and night
Far from home, far away!
I wish that spring would stay
A little longer, but fine spring
Is on the wing.
Once gone, it's left no traces.
I ask where are the flowers.
They fell with ancient rosy faces,
Whose fallen hairpins still shed
A fragrance sweet. The peach path and willowy lanes
Are dotted now with petals red.
What loving heart would for them utter sighs
But match-making bees and message-bearing butterflies,
Knocking from time to time at window-panes?

The eastern garden in a shroud
Of dark green cloud,
The deep silence beneath
The deflowered tree is broken by the sighs I breathe.
Its long thorned branches pull at my sleeves
As if to tell me how the flowers' parting grieves.
I try to pin a little flower not yet dead
To the turban on my head,
But it's unlike one on a golden hairpin new,
Shivering and beckoning to you.
O roses, do not drift away
With tide or ebb by night or day!
On broken petals red, I fear,
There's message for a lover dear.

正是换上单衣试饮新酒的大好时节，却恨一直客居异地，只能眼睁睁地看着光阴急匆匆地从指间悄悄溜走，让我白白地虚掷了许多的岁月。

繁花似锦的日子里，但愿春天能够为我暂且停留片刻，可春天却像没有听到我的祈祷一样，依然步履匆匆地归去，恰似鸟儿飞离枝头一般，一去便了无痕迹。

试问蔷薇花儿今何在？夜里的一场疾风骤雨，生生埋葬了堪与楚国宫城里那些倾国倾城的佳丽相媲美的花儿，怎不惹人心惊？落花就像美人发间坠地的钗钿，散发着残留的香气，凌乱地点缀着桃花小径，轻轻地在杨柳街巷翻飞。多情的人儿，有谁会来替这缤纷的落英惋惜？也只有那些无所事事的蜂儿蝶儿，仿佛媒人使者般，时时都殷勤叩击着窗槅，来传递心间的情意。

终是不忍辜负了这片春光，只身来到了东园，却不意东园里一片寂静，花事亦已接近尾声，好不让人惆怅。草木繁盛，渐已成荫，四下里一片青碧之色，眼看着这花团锦簇的春天也终将归于虚无。

环绕着珍贵的蔷薇花丛静静徘徊，唯有一声声叹息，不停地在耳边盘旋萦绕。蔷薇伸着长长的枝条，故意钩着行人的衣裳，做出一副牵衣、期待与之交谈的模样，对我表现出无限的依恋与离情别绪，更惹我无限的怜惜。

俯身，拣拾起一朵小小的残花，勉强簪在头巾上，却发现，终究不似一朵鲜花戴在美人发间的钗头上那般颤动、摇曳，总是俏媚地斜斜倚向春风里。花儿啊花儿，切莫随着潮汐远远地飘逝而去，只怕那些破碎的花瓣上，依旧还写着寄托相思的字句，从今后，再也无人能够有缘与之邂逅。

这阕词并非泛泛地吟咏落花，不仅抒发了对花落后的追惜之情，也抒发了对自己光阴虚掷的追惜之情。词写得极富特色，与苏轼的《水龙吟·次韵章质夫杨花词》，有着异曲同工之妙，颇值一读。

玉楼春·红酥肯放琼苞碎

李清照

红酥肯放琼苞碎，探著南枝开遍未。
不知酝藉几多香，但见包藏无限意。
道人憔悴春窗底，闷损阑干愁不倚。
要来小酌便来休，未必明朝风不起。

Spring in Jade Pavilion

Li Qingzhao

The red mume blossoms let their jade-like buds unfold.
Try to see if all sunny branches are in flower!
I do not know how much fragrance they enfold,
But I see the infinite feeling they embower.

You say I languish by the window without glee,
Reluctant to lean on the rails, laden with sorrow.
Come if you will to drink a cup of wine with me!
Who knows if the wind won't spoil the flowers tomorrow?

初开的红梅花瓣，宛如红色的凝脂，鲜嫩的梅蕊更像琼玉一般温润剔透。试问那幸运的南枝，你的花儿是否已经开遍在春天里？我不知道它究竟包含着多少幽香，只觉得它蕴藏着无限深厚的情意。

春日里的窗户底下，有人暗自忧伤憔悴，愁闷得连栏杆都懒得再去倚靠。姐妹们，想要来饮酒赏梅的话便来吧，等到明天的话，说不定就要起风了呢。

李清照这阕《玉楼春》，当属咏梅词中的佼佼者，不仅写活了梅花，也写活了赏梅者虽愁闷至极，却仍然禁不住想要及时赏梅的矛盾心态。

这阕词应当作于宋徽宗崇宁前期，陈祖美《李清照简明年表》判断此词作于崇宁三年（1104年）。在此期间，李清照曾上诗公爹赵挺之，请救其父李格非。当时新旧党争非常激烈，李清照为党祸所左右，时居汴京，时返原籍，心境自是凄楚悲怆。

李清照（1084年—约1151年），号易安居士，齐州章丘（今山东省济南市章丘西北）人。南宋杰出的女词人，婉约派代表人物，有“千古第一才女”之称。

鹧鸪天·桂花

李清照

暗淡轻黄体性柔，情疏迹远只香留。
何须浅碧深红色，自是花中第一流。
梅定妒，菊应羞，画阑开处冠中秋。
骚人可煞无情思，何事当年不见收。

Partridge in the Sky
To the Laurel Flower
Li Qingzhao

You are so tender, though of pale, light yellow hue;
Far from caress of heart and hand, fragrant are you.
How can you need the color of rose and green jade?
Beside you there're no beautiful flowers but fade.

Envious mumes should grow;
Chrysanthemums feel shy;
By balustrade you blow
Under mid-autumn sky.
The poet Qu must be insensible of your beauty,
Or how could he neglect to praise you as was his duty?

美丽的桂花，色泽浅黄暗淡，形貌温顺又娇羞。最妙的是，它性情萧疏，远离尘世，唯有清幽的香气经久不衰，长久地留存于世。无须用浅绿或大红的色相去招摇卖弄，它本来就是花中的第一流上品。

梅花肯定会妒忌它，而它又足以令迟开的菊花感到害羞。在装有华丽护栏的花园里，它在中秋的应时花木中更是无双无俦，冠绝一时。大诗人屈原啊，可真叫无情无义，在写到诸多花木的《离骚》里，为何偏偏不见他把桂花收进去呢？

这阕词作于建中靖国（1101 年）之后，词人与丈夫赵明诚居住在青州之时。

由于北宋末年党争的牵累，李清照的公公赵挺之死后，她曾随夫长期屏居乡间。摆脱了官场上的钩心斗角，远离了都市的喧嚣纷扰，在归来堂悉心研玩金石书画，给他们的隐退生活，带来了蓬勃的生机和无穷的乐趣。他们攻读而忘名，自乐而远利，双双沉醉于美好、和谐的艺术天地中，此词便是在这种历史背景下创作的。

清平乐·忆吴江赏木樨

辛弃疾

少年痛饮，忆向吴江醒。明月团团高树影，十里水沉烟冷。

大都一点宫黄，人间直恁(nèn)芬芳。怕是秋天风露，染教世界都香。

Pure Serene Music
To Laurel Flowers Enjoyed at Wujiang
Xin Qiji

While young, I drank till drunk, awake from dream,
I remember I found in face the Southern Stream.
The full moon cast your shadow all around
On mist-veiled water deep, flowing without a sound.

Only a yellow dot of mirth
Spreads so much fragrance on earth.
Dyed in autumn breeze and dew,
You would give the whole world a perfume new.

少年的我，曾在这里狂饮过一场，还记得，那时酒醒之后，呈现在眼前的便是那奔流不息的吴淞江。抬头望去，团团明月投下了桂树的高大身影，十里之外都散溢着桂花的幽香。

大多的桂花都只不过有一点点宫黄之色，并没有什么特别之处，可它偏生给人间送来了这般别致的芬芳。想来，兴许就是它要借着秋天的风露，让这清幽的香气飘散到四面八方，让整个世界都迅即变香吧！

这是辛弃疾闲居上饶时，与他的朋友余叔良互相唱和时所作的一阕词。余叔良履历不详，只知辛弃疾与他互有唱酬，其中《沁园春·答余叔良》云：“我试评君，君定何如，玉川似之。”由此便可知其是辛弃疾身边一位声气相应的朋友。

辛弃疾自隆兴二年（1164 年）冬，或乾道元年（1165 年）春，江阴签判任满后，曾有一段流寓吴江的生活，此词所回忆的时期，当是辛弃疾向朝廷进献《美芹十论》之后，这正是他希望一展宏图的时候。

辛弃疾（1140 年—1207 年），原字坦夫，后改字幼安，中年后别号稼轩，济南历城（今山东省济南市历城区）人。南宋著名将领、文学家，豪放派词人，有“词中之龙”之称。与苏轼合称“苏辛”，与李清照并称“济南二安”。

木兰花令·柳

王观

铜驼陌上新正后，第一风流除是柳。
勾牵春事不如梅，断送离人强似酒。
东君有意偏挼(ruán)就，惯得腰肢真个瘦。
阿谁道你不思量，因甚眉头长恁皱。

Song of Magnolia Flower

Wang Guan

On the pathway after the spring day
The first to waft in breeze are willow trees,
Not so attractive to spring as mume blooms divine
But to those who part more heart-breaking than wine.

The Sun God in the East has for you a love tender;
He's fond of your waist slender.
No lady could forget you now
When she unknits her leaf-like brow.

洛阳城南的铜驼街上，在新春正月到来后，最显得俊俏风流的，便是那叶芽青嫩、柔条迎风而舞的柳树了。柳虽得春意之先，但人们却常以梅为东风第一枝，生生地让柳逊了梅一筹。而在送别的场合，柳的作用则远远大于美酒，当然也就更胜于梅了。

掌管春天的神明东君，似乎也特别地宠爱和迁就柳树，以至娇纵得它的腰肢，一如既往地纤瘦，绵软得就跟没有骨头的支撑一样。风流多情的柳树，恰似痴情的女子，总是因为对离人的思量，终日里皱着眉头，却又不知道它心里到底在恋慕着何人。

这阕词从表面上看是在咏柳，实则借柳喻人，通过对柳的描绘，以轻松活泼、清丽明快的笔触，塑造了一个风尘女子的形象，寄予了词人对她的同情与赞美。

王观的词，工细轻柔，清新脱俗，而又尽显自然，王灼在《碧鸡漫志》中称赞他说："其新丽处与轻狂处皆足惊人。"确非妄语。他的词作，与柳永的作品有某些类同之处，本篇即鲜明地体现了这一艺术特色。

王观（1035 年—1100 年），字通叟，号逐客，泰州如皋（今江苏省南通市如皋）人，与秦观并称"二观"。

宋仁宗嘉祐二年（1057 年）中进士，后历任大理寺丞、江都知县等。相传曾奉诏作《清平乐》词一阕，描写宫廷生活。高太后因对王安石变法不满，认为王观是王安石门生，就以《清平乐》亵渎了宋神宗为名，第二天便将王观罢职，此后，王观便自号"逐客"。

代表作有《卜算子·送鲍浩然之浙东》《临江仙·离怀》《高阳台》等，其中《卜算子》一词以水喻眼波，以山指眉峰，设喻巧妙，又语带双关，写得妙趣横生，堪称杰作。

第四章

清愁×自醉

CHAPTER FOUR

I can but drink to drown

苏幕遮·草

梅尧臣

露堤平，烟墅杳。乱碧萋萋，雨后江天晓。独有庾(yǔ)郎年最少。窣地春袍，嫩色宜相照。

接长亭，迷远道。堪怨王孙，不记归期早。落尽梨花春又了。满地残阳，翠色和烟老。

Waterbag Dance

Mei Yaochen

Level banks wet with dew,
Mist-veiled cots out of view,
Green grass runs riot;
After the morning rain the river's quiet.
Only the official youngest in years,
Whose green gown caressing the ground, appears
To rival with the grass in tender hue.

It overspreads the pavilion of adieu,
And veils the lane stretched far away.
How can I not complain of my dear friend
Who's gone and won't return on an early day?
When all pear blossoms fall, spring has come to an end.
The land is steeped in the sun's departing ray,
The green grass will grow old with the smoke grey.

平坦的堤坝上，露珠在芳草上兀自滚来滚去；远处的房舍，在烟霭的掩映下若隐若现。凝眸处，雨后的天色已然放晴，江面更显开阔，而江边，则是铺天盖地、到处疯长的乱草，只看得人眼花缭乱。

离乡宦游的才子，像庾信一样年少成名，自是志得意满、满心欢喜。他穿着曳地的青色长袍，章服的颜色与嫩绿的草色互相映衬，显得十分相宜，怎一个潇洒形容得尽。

萋萋的芳草，把路边一个又一个的长亭紧密地联结在一起，让所有的路人都望不穿远处道路的尽头究竟是在哪里。要问它为什么总是长满了堤岸，还不得怪怨那宦游的王孙公子，若不是他早就忘记了归期，它又怎会绵延不休，没完没了？

眼瞅着枝头的梨花，都默默凋谢在风中，又一个春天马上就要过去，心里又蓦地生起了一股惆怅。日落黄昏，暮霭沉沉，看夕阳的余晖缓缓洒落在堤坝上，那翠绿的春草，似乎也都跟着岁月的烟尘，瞬间便苍老了许多。

宋代吴曾《能改斋漫录》卷十七《乐府·咏草词》记录了一段有关此词的故事：梅圣俞在欧阳公座，有以林逋草词“金谷年年，乱生青草谁为主”为美者。圣俞因别为《苏幕遮》一阕，“露堤平”云云，欧公击节赏之。

梅尧臣（1002年—1060年），字圣俞，北宋诗人。宣州宣城（今安徽省宣城市宣州区）人，因宣城古名宛陵，故世人又称之为宛陵先生。

初试不第，以荫补河南主簿。宋仁宗皇祐三年（1051年）召试，赐进士出身，为太常博士。以欧阳修荐，为国子监直讲，累迁尚书都官员外郎，世称梅都官。

诗主平淡，多反映现实生活和民生疾苦，以矫宋初空洞靡丽之文风。与苏舜钦齐名，世称“苏梅”。著有《宛陵先生文集》。

幽兰旋老，杜若还生，水乡尚寄旅。别后访、六桥无信，事往花委，瘗yì玉埋香，几番风雨。长波妒盼，遥山羞黛，渔灯分影春江宿。记当时、短楫桃根渡，青楼仿佛。临分败壁题诗，泪墨惨淡尘土。

危亭望极，草色天涯，叹鬓侵半苎。暗点检，离痕欢唾，尚染鲛绡，亸duǒ凤迷归，破鸾慵舞。殷勤待写，书中长恨，蓝霞辽海沉过雁。漫相思、弹入哀筝柱。伤心千里江南，怨曲重招，断魂在否？

莺啼序·春晚感怀

吴文英

残寒正欺病酒，掩沉香绣户。燕来晚、飞入西城，似说春事迟暮。画船载、清明过却，晴烟冉冉吴宫树。念羁情、游荡随风，化为轻絮。

十载西湖，傍柳系马，趁娇尘软雾。溯红渐、招入仙溪，锦儿偷寄幽素。倚银屏、春宽梦窄，断红湿、歌纨金缕。暝堤空，轻把斜阳，总还鸥鹭。

Prelude to Orioles' Warble
Recall with Emotion in the Spring Evening

Wu Wenying

Drunkenness aggravated by lingering cold,
I close the window incense-perfumed.
The swallows coming late
Fly to the western town
As if complaining spring's grown old.
After the Mourning Day
I sail a painted boat and see green willows sway
Before the ancient palace gate,
Veiled in light smoke and by sunbeams illumed.
My sorrow wafting in wind turns to willow down.

For ten long years around West Lake I've roved;
Tethered my horse to willow green
Or rode in the fine dust raised by breeze light.
I passed through flowers red,
Invited to a fairy stream
Where my songstress beloved,
Hastened my feet
By secret letter sweet.
She leaned against the silvery screen,
Long was the vernal night,
But short our dream.
Wet petals reddened silk fan and robe of gold thread.
The dusk-deserted bank was cool,
Leaving the slanting sun to heron and gull.

The fragrant orchid has grown old,

The lonely cuckoo flower cold
By waterside remain.
Since her departure I
Visit again Six Bridges in vain;
With withered flowers the past has gone by.
Her deeply buried jade-like bone
Through wind and rain has gone.
The waves still envy glance of her amorous eye;
Compared with her green brows, the distant hills feel shy.
The fisher's lamp remembers the shadows we cast
On vernal river in the past;
At Ferry of Peach Flower
Our oars did ripple shadow of her bower.
When we two parted, I wrote lines on broken wall,
But now my dreary tears and dust have blurred them all.

I look afar from tower high:
An endless green spreads far and nigh.
Over my hair half grey I sigh.
I see in secret on silk kerchief reappears
The trace of parting grief or stain of joyful tears.
The phoenix stray won't flap its wing
Nor dance before its mirrored image nor sing.
I'd pour my grief in letter long,
But message-bearing wild geese have sunk their song
Into the boundless sea which would turn blue the cloud.
I can but let my sorrow sing
On zither string.
The long, long southern shore with it will be o'erflowed.
Could her soul be called back, awoken
By my song sung with a heart broken?

饮下过量的美酒，沉醉后正独自郁闷之际，那料峭的春日余寒偏又沁入肌骨，逼得我不得不紧紧关上雕绘的门窗，又立马在屋里燃起了沉香。迟来的燕子，缓缓飞进我位于西城的住处，兀自呢喃个不停，仿佛在叹息这个短暂的春天转瞬即逝，马上又要与之擦肩而过。

清明过后，我乘着画船在西湖中漫游，远处的山峦晴烟缭绕，宫馆台苑掩映在浓密幽深的绿树之中，自是美得不可方物。回想起这些年客居他乡的情形，那千丝万缕的离情别绪，却又都跟随着眼前飘拂的春风，瞬间化为轻扬的柳絮，不知道飞到哪里去了。

这十余年来，我长期驻留在京师临安，时常把马系在西湖边的柳树上，尽情地观赏湖上柔媚的风光，怎一个欢喜了得？还记得，我曾乘着小舟，沿着红花夹岸的小溪逆流而上，渐渐地走向通往仙境的道路，而那里便是你藏身的香闺之处。

你叫侍儿为我递简传书，把满腔的柔情暗暗地倾诉。在镶银的屏风深处，我俩曾有过多少难以言说的欢乐？只可惜，春长梦短，聚会的时日总是那么仓促，每到离别之际，又总会让和着胭脂的泪水，不期然地浸透手中的纨扇和绣金的衣服。

暮色里，游人散尽，西湖两边的堤岸突地变得空空如也，我的心情也跟着变得阴晴不定。日落黄昏，夕照中波光潋滟的西湖，又把那一抹清丽的风光，通通还给了湖上的沙鸥白鹭，哪里还容得下我这满腹的思念？

岁月匆匆流逝，飘逸着幽香的兰花，转眼间便即老去，汀州上新生的杜若散溢着铺天盖地的香气，一切都还是当初的模样，而我亦依旧漂泊在河湖纵横的他乡，继续过着寄人篱下的羁旅生活。

自与你离别之后，我曾经寻访过六桥故地，却又始终得不到有关你的任何讯息。鲜花已经枯萎，从前的欢会已成陈迹，无情的风雨苦苦摧折着你，你就像那香艳珍奇的花朵，才绽放不久便即永远凋落成泥，再也无法回到我的身边。

湖面倒映着星星点点的渔火，今晚，我便独自枕着这一泓春江水，宿住在你我曾经一起居留的湖畔小屋。放眼望去，这清澈的流水，没有你含情的眼睛明丽，那苍翠葱郁的远山，更不如你弯弯的双眉秀美，只是，转身而过后，那双顾盼生辉的美目和弯如初月的秀眉，现如今又到哪里去了呢？

当年在渡口依依惜别的情景，至今依旧清晰如昨地印在我的记忆里，丝毫不曾忘却。你住过的妆楼，里面的陈设，似乎还一如往昔，而我却再也无处将你寻觅。分手时我曾在断壁残垣上为你题写下动情的诗句，而今，那和着泪水的墨痕早已蒙上了灰暗的尘土，字迹也变得模糊不清，唯有惨淡二字，才能形容得尽。

登上高亭，极目遥望，我看见远处绵延不绝的芳草，依旧像从前一样，缓缓染绿了天边的道路，此情此景，怎不让我顿生蹉跎之感？别的不说，就这半头苎麻一样苍白的鬓发，便足以让人一叹再叹。

默默翻检起当日的旧物，心里又涌起一丝莫名的哀伤。你留下的丝帕，还沾带着斑斑泪痕、点点香唾；你留下的凤钗，钗头上那只垂下羽翼的孤凤，仿若迷失了归路的孩子一样迷茫无助；你留下的鸾镜已经破碎成了满地铺陈的忧伤，镜背雕刻的那只孤独的鸾鸟，因为失去了主人的怜惜，亦已慵懒得再也不愿临风起舞了。

我满怀深情地，打算把盘桓心中的绵绵离恨，都写成一纸长长的书信，寄给擦肩而过的你，遗憾的是，鸿雁已飞过布满蓝色云霞的天空，沉入辽阔的大海深处，又有谁来为我传达这满腹的情愫？

想你，念你，我只好把这徒然的相思和无尽的愁苦，一一弹进那无限哀怨的筝曲中。再回首，千里江南，处处触景伤心，你的离魂是否就徜徉在近处，又可否能听到我哀怨的筝曲，正如泣如诉地将你追思了千遍万遍？

《莺啼序》词调，始见于《梦窗词》，实为吴文英首创。这阕《莺啼序·春晚感怀》当作于宋理宗宝祐初年，为词人悼念亡妾之作。创作此词的时候，作者应当不在杭州，而是身处苏州，因春暮而愁，回想前尘往事，感怀发兴。

据夏承焘《吴梦窗系年》："梦窗在苏州曾纳一妾，后遭遣去。在杭州亦纳一妾，后则亡殁。集中怀人诸作，其时夏秋，其地苏州者，殆皆忆苏州遣妾；其时春，其地杭州者，则悼杭州亡妾。"

刘永济《微睇室说词》："考梦窗生平最使之难忘者，乃寓吴时曾纳一妾。此妾于淳祐四年（1244年）遣去，其因何被遣，则不可得知。遣妾之后，在杭复眷一妾。此妓似未及成娶，不久既殁，其因何未及成娶，亦不可知。此词之作，在妓殁之后。梦窗老年独客，追念往事，情不能已，故有此缠绵往复之词，正姜夔所谓'少年情事老来悲'也。陈洵说此词专主去妾，则无以解释'瘗玉埋香'及'怨曲重招，断魂在否'之语。杨铁夫又于去妾之外，亡妓之后，增一楚妓，愈加胶葛矣。今定为怀去妾与悲亡妓，似较妥当。"

吴文英（约1200年—约1260年），字君特，号梦窗，晚号觉翁。四明（今浙江省宁波市）人，终生不仕，曾在江苏、浙江一带当过幕僚。南宋词人。

他的词上承温庭筠，近师周邦彦，在辛弃疾、姜夔词之外，自成一格。注重音律，长于炼字，雕琢工丽，张炎《词源》说他的词"如七宝楼台，眩人眼目，拆碎下来，不成片段"，而尹焕《花庵词选引》则认为"求词于吾宋，前有清真，后有梦窗"。

玉蝴蝶·望处雨收云断

柳永

望处雨收云断，凭阑悄悄，目送秋光。晚景萧疏，堪动宋玉悲凉。水风轻，蘋花渐老，月露冷、梧叶飘黄。遣情伤。故人何在，烟水茫茫。

难忘，文期酒会，几孤风月，屡变星霜。海阔山遥，未知何处是潇湘。念双燕、难凭远信，指暮天、空识归航。黯相望。断鸿声里，立尽斜阳。

Jade Butterfly

Liu Yong

No rain nor clouds in sight,
Silent on rails I lean
To see off late autumn serene.
Lonely in the evening twilight,
Even the ancient poet would feel sad and cold.
The water rippled by the breeze,
The duckweed gradually grows old.
The dew shed by the moon would freeze
And yellow waft the plane-tree leaves.
How longing grieves!
Where is now my old friend?
Far and wide mist and waves extend.

Can I forget
The verse-composing and wine-drinking when we met?
How many moonlit nights were passed in vain?
How often stars and frost have changed again?
The sky is wide, the sea is far,
I cannot go to River Xiao Xiang where you are.
A pair of swallows fly.
Could they bring me a letter from you?
I point to evening sky.
To what avail returns the sail I knew?
At dusk I gaze far, far away
Until I hear no more wild geese's song.
I stand there long
Until the sun has shed all its departing ray.

放眼望去，雨已停歇，云已散去，我倚着栏杆，悄悄目送着这片温润的秋色，一点一点地，缓缓消逝于天边。

秋天的傍晚，景色萧瑟荒芜，总会让人不由自主地生发出宋玉的悲秋之叹。微风低低地拂过水面，触目所及之处，白蘋花渐渐衰残，月寒露冷，梧桐叶也禁不住这寒凉的侵袭，迅即变黄，正一片片地飘落而下。

此情此景，怎不让人感伤惆怅？那些曾经的故友知交，现如今，又都沦落在何方？一切的一切，皆成过眼云烟，唯有一片一望无垠的秋水，一缕缥缈的烟雾，依然故我地穿梭在我迷离的眼前。

文人之间的雅集，纵情欢饮的酒宴，时至今日，都还历历在目，怎么也无法忘记。离别之后，物换星移，世事屡屡变迁，究竟辜负了多少的风月时光，更加难以计算。你我相隔的距离，比海宽阔，比山遥远，自是天各一方，不辨潇湘在何方，更不知猴年马月才能与君相逢。

每一次想起你，都会让我感到凄苦彷徨，却遗憾眼前这双双飞去的燕子，是无法给故友传递讯息的。期盼故友归来，一次次地在暮色中，伸手指着遥远的天际，辨识着从远处归来的舟船，怎料得过尽千帆皆不是，回首之际才发现又是一场空等待。我默默伫立在西下的夕阳中，与四周的景致黯然相望，却只听得一声孤雁的哀鸣，缓缓飘荡在天际，经久不息。

这阕词是词人为怀念湘中故人所作。以抒情为主，把写景和叙事、忆旧和怀人、羁旅和离别、时间和空间，融为一个浑然的艺术整体，具有很强的艺术感染力。

水龙吟·咏月

晁端礼

倦游京洛风尘，夜来病酒无人问。九衢qú雪少，千门月淡，元宵灯近。香散梅梢，冻消池面，一番春信。记南楼醉里，西城宴阕，都不管、人春困。

屈指流年未几，早人惊、潘郎双鬓。当时体态，如今情绪，多应瘦损。马上墙头，纵教瞥见，也难相认。凭阑干，但有盈盈泪眼，把罗襟揾wèn。

Water Dragon's Chant

Chao Duanli

Tired of the wind and dust of the capital,
I'm sick after drinking but no one cares at all.
The thoroughfares covered with snow slight,
From door to door the moon sheds a pale light,
Near is the Lantern Day.
Fragrance spread from mume spray
And ice melt on the pool will bring
The message of spring.
I remember drinking in southern bowers
And feasting in western towns,
I was never tired of vernal hours.

Counting up, only a few years have passed,
But I'm surprised my forehead has turned grey so fast.
The beauty with her grace
After these days' ups and downs
Should turn into a lean face.
On horse or over the wall,
Could we recognize each other at all?
Leaning on balustrade, her tearful look grieves
For tears can't be wiped away by silken sleeves.

我已厌倦了官场上蝇营狗苟的生活，总是在夜里借酒消愁，却因为喝多了酒导致病体缠绵，也没个人来关心慰问我一下。

街面上的积雪并不多，淡淡的月光透过薄薄的云层照进了千家万户，眼瞅着距离元宵节闹花灯的时候又近了些。夜风送来了枝头的梅香，池塘上的薄冰已经融解，春天的讯息一天浓似一天。还记得，在南楼醉酒，在西城宴饮的时光，每一天都快活得忘乎所以，哪里还管得上什么春困不春困。

屈指算来，那些明媚生姿的欢乐，距离而今其实也没有多少年，为什么我就早早地生出了满头的白发呢？我的容貌体态已经有了很大的变化，想必你也因为长久地思念我而终日愁苦难耐，以至形貌消瘦憔悴了吧？

无情的岁月改变了彼此的容颜，眼下，即便相逢在墙头马上，恐怕也难以相认。我知道，你又在想我了，你又偎着栏杆守候着我的归期，泪眼婆娑，脉脉无语，却只能一而再、再而三地举起衣袖，默默擦去脸上的泪水。

这阕词以极其精妙的结构、声韵和语言，抒发了作者在仕途和爱情上遭遇的双重挫折，所带来的失意与苦闷，将其人生种种不得意的感慨抒发得淋漓尽致。全词情景交融，对仗工整，用墨浓淡相宜，结构疏密相间，一气呵成，读来令人一咏三叹，堪称绝妙好词。

晁端礼（1046年—1113年），字次膺，济州巨野（今山东省菏泽市巨野县）人。熙宁六年（1073年）进士，任单州城武主簿、瀛洲防御推官，历知洺州平恩县、大名府莘县。宋徽宗时为大晟府协律，政和三年卒，年六十八。

有词集《闲斋琴趣外篇》六卷存世，《全宋词补辑》另从《诗渊》辑得一首。王灼《碧鸡漫志》，谓其词“源流从柳氏来”“有佳句”“病于无韵”。

南乡子·梅花词和杨元素

苏轼

寒雀满疏篱，争抱寒柯看玉蕤rui。忽见客来花下坐，惊飞。踏散芳英落酒卮。

痛饮又能诗，坐客无毡zhān醉不知。花尽酒阑春到也，离离。一点微酸已著枝。

Song of Southern Country
Mume Blossoms for Yang Yuansu

Su Shi

On the fence perch birds feeling cold,
To view the blooms of jade they dispute for branch old.
Seeing a guest sit under flowers, they fly up
And scatter petals over his wine cup.

Writing verses and drinking wine,
The guest knows not he's not sitting on felt fine.
Wine cup dried up, spring comes with fallen flower.
Leave here! The branch has felt a little sour.

稀稀疏疏的篱笆墙上，落满了披着一身寒霜的麻雀。倏忽之间，它们又争先恐后地飞到了梅树上，叽叽喳喳地打量着白玉一样晶莹润泽的梅花。

冷不防，突地见到一群前来吃酒的客人，径直走到梅树下的酒桌边坐好。麻雀们何曾见过这样的阵势，还没等客人们把酒畅饮，一下子就惊得四处乱飞，迅即踏散了枝头的梅花，纷纷落到了客人们手中举起的酒杯里。

主人杨元素不仅酒量大得厉害，而且能够仗着醉意写得一手好诗。那些醉酒后的客人们坐在没有铺上毡子的雪地上，一个个都浑然不知，却还兴奋得手舞足蹈。

酒已饮尽，花已赏够，春天已悄然来到人间。宴会举行了一次又一次，大家喝了又喝，不知不觉间，洁白的梅花已默默爬满了枝头。

苏轼为杭州通判时，杨元素出任杭州知州，在此期间，二人结下了深厚的友谊，自此后，相互间多有唱和，而这阕梅花词便是苏轼奉和杨元素之作。此词写于宋神宗熙宁七年（1074年）冬，当时杨元素依然在杭州任上，而苏轼则已身在密州。

虞美人·波声拍枕长淮晓

苏轼

波声拍枕长淮晓，隙月窥人小。无情
汴水自东流，只载一船离恨向西州。

竹溪花浦曾同醉，酒味多于泪。谁教
风鉴在尘埃？酝造一场烦恼送人来！

The Beautiful Lady Yu

Su Shi

River Huai's waves seem to beat my pillow till dawn;
A ray of moonbeam peeps at me forlorn.
The heartless River Bian flows eastward down,
Laden with parting grief, you've left the town.

Once we got drunk by riverside bamboo and flower,
My tears made sweet wine sour.
How could a mirror not be stained with dust?
Who could predict the trouble brewing up in gust?

饮别后归卧舟中，耳边只听到淮水波声，仿若一浪一浪地拍打在枕畔，不知不觉间，天已经亮了。从船篷的缝隙中望出去，一轮残月依旧挂在天边，既小巧又玲珑，倒也可爱得很。汴水无情，伴着故人向东流去，而我却满载着一船离愁别恨，独自向扬州公廨的西门而去。

想当年，你我醉眠于竹溪花浦之间，那时欢聚畅饮的情谊，远远胜过别后的伤悲与泪水。到底，是谁让你这样才华横溢、风度翩翩，而又见识高绝的人才，一直都蒙尘于野呢？无人赏识于你，在这离别之际，平白地又给本就惆怅莫名的我，增添了一场不尽的烦恼。

宋神宗元丰七年（1084年）十一月，苏轼从扬州出发，到高邮与秦观相会。离去之际，秦观送其至淮河边，这阕词便是苏轼与秦观在淮河饮别时所作。

满庭芳·蜗角虚名

苏轼

蜗角虚名，蝇头微利，算来著甚干忙。事皆前定，谁弱又谁强。且趁闲身未老，①尽放我、些子疏狂。百年里，浑教是醉，三万六千场。

思量，能几许，忧愁风雨，一半相妨，又何须抵死，说短论长。幸对清风皓月，苔茵展、云幕高张。江南好，千钟美酒，一曲满庭芳。

①尽放我一作：须放我

Courtyard Full of Fragrance

Su Shi

For fame as vain as a snail's horn
And profit as slight as a fly's head,
Should I be busy and forlorn?
Fate rules for long,
Who is weak? Who is strong?
Not yet grown old and having leisure,
Let me be free to enjoy pleasure!
Could I be drunk in a hundred years,
Thirty-six hundred times without shedding tears?

Think how long life can last,
Though sad and harmful storms I've passed.
Why should I waste my breath
Until my death,
To say the short and long
Or right and wrong?
I am happy to enjoy clear breeze and the moon bright,
Green grass outspread
And a canopy of cloud white.
The Southern shore is fine
With a thousand cups of wine
And the courtyard fragrant with song.

蜗角一样的虚名，蝇头一样的薄利，有什么值得为之忙碌个不停呢？名利得失之事，自有前定的因缘，得者未必强，失者未必弱，更无须过分介意。赶紧趁着这闲散之身还未老去之际，彻底抛开束缚，去过那无拘无束的生活吧，哪怕人生只有一百年的时光，我也愿意大醉它三万六千场。

暗自思量，我这一生起码有一半的日子，都是在辗转流徙中度过的，见过的风雨、历经过的忧愁，多了去了，又有什么必要，非得一天到晚地说长说短呢？还不如敞开胸怀，心无旁骛地面对这清风明月，以苍苔为褥席，以高云为帷帐，无忧无虑地过好自己的生活。还是江南好啊，这里不仅有一千盅美酒，还有一曲悦耳动听的《满庭芳》，即便是神仙来了，也定然会乐不思归。

这阕《满庭芳》的具体创作时间难以确证，但从词中所表现的内容和抒发的情感来看，应是在苏轼受到重大挫折之后,大致可判断为贬于黄州之际。

齐天乐·白发

史达祖

秋风早入潘郎鬓，斑斑遽（jù）惊如许。暖雪侵梳，晴丝拂领，栽满愁城深处。

瑶簪谩妒。便羞插宫花，自怜衰暮。尚想春情，旧吟凄断茂陵女。

人间公道惟此，叹朱颜也恁，容易堕去。涅不重缁（zī），搔来更短，方悔风流相误。

郎潜几缕。渐疏了铜驼，俊游俦侣。纵有黟（yī）黟，奈何诗思苦。

Universal Joy
My White Hair

Shi Dazu

Early has the autumn breeze whitened my forehead,
I am surprised to find grey thread on thread.
My comb seems invaded by snow white,
My collar caressed by sunbeams bright,
My heart overgrown with grief will fade.
Envying my hairpin of jade,
I would feel shy to be adorned with palace flowers,
And I pity my decrepit hours.
Recalling love of yore, an old song has denied
A new bride.

Will white hair do justice then alike to all men?
I sigh:
A rosy face will lose its dye.
Dyed black, my hair will turn white again;
Scratched, it will shorter remain.
I regret to have misused my youth in gallantry.
A few wreaths alienate
My friends early and late.
Though still I have a few hairs black,
Could bitter verse to my young days turn me back?

秋风乍起，才惊觉鬓间的青丝，已如年轻的潘岳一样，在不知不觉中，早早地化作了斑驳的白发。这一根根早生的华发，恰如侵入梳齿间的暖雪，又仿佛是昆虫吐出的游丝在衣领上飘过，徒然栽得满腹的愁绪于心间。

举杯消愁愁更愁，这满头的白发，白得闪亮晃眼，就连白玉簪都心生嫉妒，却不理会我心底究竟藏了多少苦楚。光阴似箭，人生如白驹过隙，而今，早已不好意思再把那鲜艳的花儿插上发际，唯在一声声叹息里哀怜自己已到垂暮之年。还是会不由自主地想起青春岁月里的情事，之所以会遭逢种种不幸，或许也跟卓文君一样，因为年华老去，才会受到嫌弃，只能以一阕《白头吟》凄然相对。

叹，时光荏苒，红颜易老，任何人都无法永远地留住青春，人世间最最公道的事情恐怕也唯有这一桩了。这恼人的白发，就算用黑色染料也染不黑它，更兼得越搔越短越稀疏，方才明白，却原来，风流早已两两相误，却是悔之晚矣。

颜驷三世不遇，老于郎署，拙于为官的我又何尝不是？被贬出京后，我便渐渐疏于嬉游，也慢慢地断了跟昔日亲旧故交的联系。往事不堪回首，纵有满头青丝乌发，也不过都付于一腔无奈，只换得一首首充满苦涩却又全然无用的诗文罢了！

这阕词通篇使用典故，借咏物来抒情，可谓匠心独运。典故之间的横向联系，构成了叹老嗟卑、生不逢时的内容，主观意象竖向的概括，又使不可言喻的复杂感情若隐若现地流露了出来。

史达祖（生卒年不详），字邦卿，号梅溪，汴（今河南省开封市）人。南宋婉约派重要词人，风格工巧，推动宋词走向基本定型。

齐天乐·蝉

王沂孙

一襟馀恨宫魂断，年年翠阴庭树。乍咽凉柯，还移暗叶，重把离愁深诉。西窗过雨。怪瑶珮流空，玉筝调柱。镜暗妆残，为谁娇鬓尚如许。

铜仙铅泪似洗，叹携盘去远，难贮零露。病翼惊秋，枯形阅世，消得斜阳几度？余音更苦。甚独抱清高，顿成凄楚？谩想熏风，柳丝千万缕。

A Skyful of Joy
The Cicada
Wang Yisun

The cicada transformed from the wronged Queen of Qi
Pours out her broken heart from year to year on the tree.
It sobs now on cold twig and now on darkened leaves;
Again and again
It laments her death and grieves.
When the west window's swept by rain,
It sings in the air as her jasper pendant tings
Or her fair fingers play on zither's stings.
No longer black is now her mirrored hair;
I ask for whom its wings should still be black and fair.

The golden statue steeped in tears of lead
Was carried far away with plate in days of old.
Where can the cicada find dew on which it fed?
Its sickly wings are afraid of autumn cold
And its abandoned form has witnessed rise and fall.
How many sunsets can it still endure?
Its last song is saddest of all.
Why should it sing alone on high and pure
And suddenly appear
So sad and drear?
Can it forget the summer breeze
When waved thousands of twigs of willow trees?

宫妃满怀离恨，愤然魂断，化作一只哀蝉，年年都在庭院的绿荫丛中兀自哀鸣。它刚刚还在枝头上呜咽，不一会儿却又飞到幽暗的密叶丛中兀自鸣叫，一遍又一遍地，将那生离死别的满腹愁绪，向路过的人儿深深地倾诉。

西窗外秋雨初歇，蝉儿被惊动后发出的声音，仿佛玉佩在空中叮当作响，又恰似玉筝调整弦柱时撞击出的美妙动人的声乐。叹，昔日的明镜已经昏暗，妆容也已变得黯淡无光，却为何，这薄如蝉翼的鬓发还和从前那样娇美如初？

金铜仙人堕下的铅泪如同洗过一般，去国辞乡，可叹她已携盘远去，再也不能贮藏清露以供哀蝉享用了。蝉儿病弱的双翼，最是惊怕秋天的到来，那枯槁的形骸在世间已沧桑历尽，又还能承担起多少次斜阳秋寒的折磨呢？

蝉之将亡，凄楚欲断的哀鸣声，更是让人觉得悲苦异常，可为什么，它还想着要独自将这哀怨的曲调一再地吟唱，让自己在瞬息之间承受那无尽的哀伤？此时此刻，它亦只能徒然地追忆夏风吹暖、柳丝飘摇的盛景，只可惜，往日的欢乐早已不在，一切的一切都成虚无。

《花外集》和《乐府补题》中均收录了这阕词。《乐府补题》为宋遗民感愤于元僧杨琏真伽盗挖宋代帝后陵墓而作的咏物词集。词中的齐后化蝉、魏女蝉鬓，都与王室后妃有关，“为谁娇鬓尚如许”一句，很有可能关合孟后发髻。另外，金铜承露的典故，则隐射了宋亡及帝陵被盗事，咏物托意，且以意贯穿始终，无有痕迹。

解连环·孤雁

张炎

楚江空晚。怅离群万里，恍然惊散。自顾影、欲下寒塘，正沙净草枯，水平天远。写不成书，只寄得、相思一点。料因循误了，残毡拥雪，故人心眼。

谁怜旅愁荏苒。谩长门夜悄，锦筝弹怨。想伴侣、犹宿芦花，也曾念春前，去程应转。暮雨相呼，怕蓦地、玉关重见。未羞他、双燕归来，画帘半卷。

Double Rings Unchained
The Lonely wild Swallow

Zhang Yan

Over the southern stream at the close of the day,
Suddenly startled, you go astray
And from the row in flight you're miles away.
You gaze at your own image in the sandy pool
And would alight' mid withered grass by water cool.
Alone in the vast sky you cannot form a row,
So like a dot of yearning you should go.
How can you not delay
The message of the envoy eating wool
Mixed with snow!
Who would pity your loneliness?

The queen deserted, companionless,
At quiet night in Palace of Long Gate
Might play pitiful tunes on zither's string.
You may think of flowering reeds where rests your mate,
Who should come back before next spring.
What if you meet at Gate of Jade again,
Calling each other in the evening rain!
Then you won't envy swallows in pair,
Flitting by half unrolled curtain of the fair.

楚江的夜空辽阔而澄静，一只孤单的大雁正独自飞行在茫茫的暮色之中。它满怀悲怆，神情委顿，自那日被一场突如其来的变故将它与雁阵惊散后，它已脱离雁群有万里之遥了。

来也孤单，去也孤单，顾影自怜的它，犹犹豫豫着想要飞下寒塘，另寻栖身之处，却不意，触目所及之处，天苍苍，野茫茫，江面平阔，正伸向遥远的未知，唯有一片荒沙衰草，静静地徜徉在大地的怀抱。

往日的雁阵，总会排成一字形或人字形，而今，形单影只的它，却无法排成字形，只能够飞成一个小小的点，为远方的同伴寄去一点难耐的相思。怕只怕，再这样徘徊迁延下去，定然会耽误了替北地吞毡啮雪的故人寄书，无法传达他们眷念故园的心愿。

时光荏苒，有谁会怜惜它长途飞行的艰辛？凄惶中，不禁想起深夜里孤居长门宫的陈皇后，那弦柱斜列如雁阵的锦筝，弹奏出的依旧是无尽的幽怨与惆怅。想来，同伴们此刻还栖宿在南方茂密的芦花丛中吧？它们曾念叨着要在春天之前，沿着旧路飞回北方，而它，却不知道什么时候才能与它们聚首。潇潇暮雨中，它一声声地呼唤着同伴，哪怕明知道它们不可能出现在它面前。也许会出现奇迹呢？也许它们已从南方返回，就在离它不远的前方呢？它兀自欺骗着自己，之所以那么急切地想见到它们，是因为害怕突然在边塞与它们重逢，只怕到那个时候，它倒要乐极生悲了呢。

长久的期待与渴盼，让它终日惶惶不安，无所适从。眼瞅着团聚的日子越来越近，它又蓦地担心起春天会来得太快，会打乱它所有的计划。罢了罢了，还是飞到哪里算哪里的好，当百花盛开，燕子翩跹着归来，双双栖息于画帘半卷的房檐之际，一心只想着振翅远飞的它，也不必为自己会步了燕子的后尘寄人篱下而感到羞惭，不是吗？

这阕词是南宋灭亡后所作，是一篇著名的咏物佳构。表面上是咏孤雁，实则是借孤雁寄托词人的家国之痛，同时也反映出了南宋遗民的普遍生活体验及感触，具有非常典型的时代意义。

它构思巧妙，体物相当细腻。在写到孤雁外相的同时，又寄寓了深微的含意。此词将咏雁、怀人、自怜合而为一，抒发了词人的亡国之悲、漂泊之苦，读来甚是凄婉动人。

张炎（1248年—1314年后），字叔夏，号玉田，又号乐笑翁。临安（今浙江省杭州市）人，祖籍秦州成纪（今甘肃省天水市）。宋末元初著名词人，名将张俊六世孙。

祖父张濡，父亲张枢，皆能词善音律。前半生富贵无忧，1276年，元兵攻破临安，南宋覆灭，张濡被元人磔杀，家财亦被抄没，此后，家道中落，贫难自给，曾北游燕赵谋官，最终失意南归，落魄而终。著有《山中白云词》，今存词三百零二首。

双头莲·呈范至能待制

陆游

华鬓星星，惊壮志成虚，此身如寄。萧条病骥。向暗里、消尽当年豪气。梦断故国山川，隔重重烟水。身万里，旧社凋零，青门俊游谁记？

尽道锦里繁华，叹官闲昼永，柴荆添睡。清愁自醉。念此际、付与何人心事。纵有楚柁(duò)吴樯，知何时东逝？空怅望，鲙(kuài)美菰(gū)香，秋风又起。

Double Lotus
For Fan Chengda

Lu You

My forehead dotted with sparks white,
I start to find my ambition hard to fulfil,
My life as parasite.
Like a steed drear and ill,
Swallowing up my pride of bygone years, I sigh
To find my native land only in dreams,
Severed by mountains and misty streams.
I'm far away,
Few friends still stay.
Who can remember the prime of our day gone by?

Though flourishing is the Silk Town,
I have few things to do early or late,
But sleep within closed gate.
I can but drink to drown
My grief, for now in whom can I confide?
Though there's east-going boat on boat,
When can my ship begin to float?
I long in vain
For fish and food of native land by riverside,
For the west wind rises again.

双鬓已白，星星斑斑。到而今，这满腔的报国壮志已然落空，终于止不住地伤心惊叹，这一生，有的只是漂泊不定，流离失所，而这一颗报效朝廷的心，也始终无处安放。

此时此刻，我就像一匹患了病的寂寞的千里马，无可奈何地倚着槽栏，独自望向暗处，把当年冲天的豪气，一点一点地消磨殆尽。而今的我，即便在梦中，也难以再见到故国的锦绣河山，它早就让那重重的烟霭、层层的云水隔断了。身距都城有万里之遥，旧日的集社早已人消星散，谁还能记得才俊们当年在青门交游时的凌云壮志？

人人都说成都城繁华，我却感叹官职太闲，终日里无所事事，白天仿佛永远都过不完一样，无聊得只想把柴门紧闭，一个人躲在屋子里美美地睡上一觉。美酒浇灭不了满心的愁绪，这满腹的愁绪无处可诉，无人可诉，每每念及于此，倒又让我陷入了无尽的醉意，奈之若何？

此愁无计可消，心事无人可托，既如此，还不如及早归乡的好！只是，纵然有驶向家乡的船只，我又哪里能知道它们什么时候才会启程东下呢？我只能携着满怀的惆怅，借着一缕乍然而起的秋风，透过千万里的迢遥，在想象中望向家乡鲜嫩的鲈鱼，还有那喷香的菰菜。

宋孝宗淳熙二年（1175年）秋，陆游在成都范成大府中为官时，因感到壮志成空，北伐大业遥遥无期，现任官职又十分闲散无聊，遂终日沉湎于诗酒，故而想向老朋友倾诉心里的郁闷，便写下了这阕词。

陆游（1125年—1210年），字务观，号放翁，越州山阴（今浙江省绍兴市）人。尚书右丞陆佃之孙，南宋著名文学家、史学家、爱国诗人。

陆游一生笔耕不辍，诗词文俱取得相当高的成就。其诗语言平易晓畅，章法整饬谨严，兼具李白的雄奇奔放与杜甫的沉郁悲凉，尤以饱含爱国热情，对后世产生了深远的影响。其词与散文成就亦高，宋人刘克庄谓其词“激昂慷慨者，稼轩不能过”。

鹊桥仙·夜闻杜鹃

陆游

茅檐人静，蓬窗灯暗，春晚连江风雨。林莺巢燕总无声，但月夜、常啼杜宇。

催成清泪，惊残孤梦，又拣深枝飞去。故山犹自不堪听，况半世、飘然羁旅！

Immortal at the Magpie Bridge Hearing the Cuckoo's Cry at Night

Lu You

Under the thatched eaves all's still at night;
By the straw window flickers candlelight,
While wind and rain o'erspread the river in late spring.
Nor orioles nor swallows in their nests will sing,
But I hear the cuckoo's cry
Oft rend the moonlit sky.

Urging clear tears to stream
And startling me from lonely dream,
Away to a deep-hidden branch they fly.
Even in native hills I could not stand their song,
Let alone after half my life drifting along.

低矮的茅屋里，寂静得听不到任何的声音；简陋的篷窗下，灯火昏暗，摇曳不定。这春日的夜晚，远处的江面上偏生又风雨连天，怎不叫人愁绪丛生。林间的黄莺和燕子都停止了鸣叫，唯有杜鹃，还时常在月夜里发出阵阵哀啼，一声声，只叫得人肝肠寸断。

杜鹃凄厉的啼叫，瞬间惊醒了我的孤梦，催落我两行清泪，而它却又拣着深枝飞远了，根本就不在意我的忧伤、我的痛苦。在故乡的时候，犹自不堪听闻杜鹃凄苦的啼鸣，更何况而今已年过半百、一直都漂泊在羁旅路上的我。

宋孝宗乾道八年（1172 年）冬，陆游离开南郑（今陕西省汉中市南郑区），于第二年春赴成都任职，之后又在西川淹留了六年。总的来说，这段时期的他是郁郁不得志的，心情本来就不好，再加上“夜闻杜鹃”，自然会惊动敏感的心弦而思绪万千。据夏承焘《放翁词编年笺注》，这阕词当作于陆游客居四川的这段时间。

木兰花·立春日作

陆游

三年流落巴山道，破尽青衫尘满帽。
身如西瀼渡头云，愁抵瞿塘关上草。
春盘春酒年年好，试戴银旛判醉倒。
今朝一岁大家添，不是人间偏我老。

瀼 ràng　瞿 qú　旛 fān

Magnolia Flower
Spring Day
Lu You

A roamer from the east to the west for three years,
Worn out in my blue gown, dusty my hat appears.
Like floating cloud over the ferry of west stream,
Or grass overgrown in Three Gorges, my grief would seem.

From year to year spring plate is as good as spring wine;
We vie to be drunk adorned with ribbons fine.
All of us have grown older by one year today;
I'm not the only one to olden in my way.

屈指数来，不知不觉间，我流落在大巴山一带，已经有三年时间了。遗憾的是，到如今，我还是一袭破青衫穿了又穿，帽子上也沾满了尘土，穷困又潦倒，只身沦落在天涯。叹，身似西瀼水渡口上的浮云，愁如瞿塘峡中的春草除去还生，这样的日子，何时才是个尽头？

春盘春酒年年都丰盛如斯，醇香醉人，一到立春之日，我便又会像往年一样，在发间戴上银旛胜，然后，不管不顾地痛饮一番，一直喝到醉倒为止。人间众生，到今日，都算痴长了一岁，绝非偏偏只有我一人走向衰老。

这阕词作于宋孝宗乾道七年（1171 年）岁末立春之时，当时陆游已年届四十七岁，在四川任夔州通判。

全词抑郁之情贯穿始终，而上下两片乍看起来，却像是两幅图画、两种情怀。上片表现了一个忧国伤时、穷愁潦倒的悲剧人物形象，下片展现的却是一个头戴银旛、醉态可掬的喜剧人物形象，两片表现手法截然相异，构思布局错综复杂，显示出了词人高超的艺术水平。

天仙子·水调数声持酒听

时为嘉禾小倅，以病眠，不赴府会。

张先

水调数声持酒听，午醉醒来愁未醒。
送春春去几时回？临晚镜，伤流景，
往事后期空记省。
沙上并禽池上暝，云破月来花弄影。
重重帘幕密遮灯，风不定，人初静，
明日落红应满径。

Song of the Immortal

Zhang Xian

Wine cup in hand, I listen to Water Melody;
Awake from wine at noon, but not from melancholy.
When will spring come back now it is going away?
In the mirror, alas!
I see happy time pass.
In vain may I recall the old days gone for aye.

Night falls on poolside sand where pairs of lovebirds stay;
The moon breaks through the clouds, with shadows flowers play.
Lamplights veiled by screen on screen can't be seen.
The fickle wind still blows;
The night so silent grows.
Tomorrow fallen reds should cover the pathway.

写这阕词的时候，我还是嘉禾县的通判小吏，因病而眠，未曾去官府办公。

我手执酒杯，一边喝着酒，一边听着《水调歌》。午间吃了几杯酒后便昏昏睡了过去，醒来后，醉意虽然消了，但愁绪却未曾有过半分消解。

就这么送走了春天，可春天何时才会再回来呢？临近傍晚，我兀自举起镜子照了起来，却叹年华已老，只能在惆怅与惋惜声里，默默感伤那些逝去的光阴，还有那些如烟的往事，总是在时过境迁后，空自让人沉吟。

鸳鸯于黄昏后，交颈并眠在池边的沙洲上；花枝在冲破云层的月光下，舞弄着自己的倩影。一重又一重的帘幕，密密地遮住了灯光，风儿还没有停歇，人已经彻底安静了下来，想必明日的落花，定然会铺满这园中的小径。

根据词前小序，作者写这阕词的时候，正在嘉禾（今浙江省嘉兴市）担任判官小吏。按照沈祖棻《宋词赏析》的说法，张先在嘉禾做判官，约在宋仁宗庆历元年（1041 年），年五十二。但词中所写情事，与小序内容很不相干，所以这段小序可能是诗人偶记词乃何地何时所作，却被误认为词题，并流传了下来。

沁园春·寒食郓州道中

谢枋得

十五年来，逢寒食节，皆在天涯。叹雨濡露润，还思宰柏，风柔日媚，羞见飞花。麦饭纸钱，只鸡斗酒，几误林间噪喜鸦。天笑道，此不由乎我，也不由他。

鼎中炼熟丹砂。把紫府清都作一家。想前人鹤驭，常游绛阙，浮生蝉蜕，岂恋黄沙。帝命守坟，王令修墓，男子正当如是耶。又何必，待过家上冢，昼锦荣华。

Spring in a Pleasure Garden On Cold Food Day

Xie Fangde

For fifteen years, on Cold Food Day,
I have roamed far away.
I sigh when dew falls or it rains hard.
Can I not think of the cypress in the graveyard?
When the wind's soft and the sun bright,
I feel ashamed to see flowers in plight.
The paper money, wheat and rice,
Chicken and wine can't be offered for sacrifice.
Hungry are hovering magpies and crows in flight.
In laughter Heaven said,
"I'm not to blame, nor are you at all."

When in the tripod the elixir's made,
I'd fly to the palace of Taoist capital.
Think of the immortal who on the crane's back flew
To the celestial hall!
With yellow sand I will no more fall in love
Than a cicada with its slough.
I'm ordered to guard
The imperial graveyard
Is it what a man should properly do?
Why should I forsake the old for the new,
To live in a vainglorious hue?

这十五年以来，每逢寒食节，我都没有回过故乡，而是一个人孤孤单单地流浪在天涯海角。在阴雨连绵的天气里，我思念着祖宗坟茔上的柏树；在风和日丽的天气里，却又羞于见到飞花。我不能在寒食节回到故乡，为祖宗供奉麦饭、烧纸钱，更无法为他们准备祭祀用的鸡肉和美酒，就连那盘旋在林间等候享用祭食的喜鹊和乌鸦，也都白白地空等了。这到底是为什么呢？老天爷笑着说：这不是因为我，也不是因为元军的入侵。

我早就看破生死，也早就为自己的后事想好了退路。现如今，我就像那鼎中炼熟的丹砂，随时都可以升天而去，从此后，便以紫府清都为家，做一个逍遥自在的神仙。想那从前的仙人，时常驾鹤游于天上的绛阙，世俗之身如同金蝉脱壳般，被毫不吝惜地丢弃，又岂会留恋这尘埃浊世？大宋皇帝命令臣子替先帝守坟、修葺墓园，好儿郎就应当好好听命报效于君王，又何必等到奉命回家上坟祭祖的时候，在乡人面前彰显那不值一提的荣华富贵？

这阕词是谢枋得过郓州（今山东省菏泽市郓城县）时所作。宋朝灭亡之后，元朝不断南下征伐，其间，词人一直隐居在闽中，直到至元二十六年（1289年），元统治者强行逼他北上，他才不得不行，因中途遇寒食节，遂有感写下此词。词人四月抵达燕京，但最终绝食而死，年六十四岁。

谢枋得（1226年—1289年），字君直，号叠山，信州弋阳（今江西省上饶市弋阳县）人。宝祐四年（1256年）进士，曾任江西招谕使，知信州（今江西省上饶市）。宋亡之后，隐居闽中，后福建参政魏天佑为取媚于金廷，强执谢枋得北上，至大都，绝食而死。有《叠山集》存世。

第五章

山河×故人

CHAPTER FIVE

Old friends from the mountains and rivers

归朝欢·和苏坚伯固

苏轼

我梦扁舟浮震泽。雪浪摇空千顷白。觉来满眼是庐山，倚天无数开青壁。

此生长接淅。与君同是江南客。梦中游，觉来清赏，同作飞梭掷。

明日西风还挂席。唱我新词泪沾臆。灵均去后楚山空，澧阳兰芷无颜色。

君才如梦得。武陵更在西南极。《竹枝词》，莫徭yáo新唱，谁谓古今隔。

Happy Return to the Court
In Reply to Su Jian

Su Shi

I dream my leaflike boat on the vast lake afloat,
Snowlike waves surge up for miles and whiten the air.
I wake to find Mount Lu resplendent to my eye,
Blue cliffs upon blue cliffs open against the sky.
I've suffered setbacks all my life long;
You and I sing alike the roamer's song.
Dreaming of boating on the lake,
I like the thrilling scene when awake,
And feel as happy as the shuttle flies.

You will set sail in western breeze tomorrow;
I'll croon in tears for you a new verse full of sorrow.
When Poet Qu is gone, the Southern Mountain's bare.
Sweet orchids and clovers will lose their hue
Like the poet of Willow Branch Song, you
Will go farther southwest.
But you may compose as a guest.
And then who says
The modern age cannot surpass the bygone days?

我曾梦见与你同舟游于太湖，雪白的浪花一望无垠，正兀自在天际间翻空摇舞。梦醒之后，满眼里都是庐山的绮丽风光，但见千峰峭峙，直插云霄，草木青葱，蔚然深秀。

这一生，行色匆匆，总是在四处漂泊流浪，而今又与你同作江南过客，怎一个唏嘘形容得尽？叹，梦中所游历的地方，还有眼前所见的湖光山色，终不过俱如飞梭过眼，转瞬即逝。

想到明天还要扬帆西去，忍不住泪眼婆娑地唱起了我新写的词句，却是越唱越惆怅。自打屈原离开后，楚地再无人才，澧阳的香草也失去了往昔的清芬与光泽。你的才华和刘禹锡比起来，相差无几，他谪居的武陵在这里的西南方向，又和你要去的澧阳同是莫徭族人聚居之地，待到了那里，你便可以接续刘禹锡的衣钵，创作出可与《竹枝词》媲美的“莫徭新唱”来，若真能那样，谁人又能再说出古今有隔的话来呢？

元祐四年（1089 年），苏轼守杭州，与手下属官苏坚成为好友。三年后，苏坚离杭归乡，苏轼写了一阕《青玉案》为他送别。

宋哲宗绍圣元年（1094 年）六月，苏轼遭弹劾，被贬英州（今广东省英德市），还没到英州就又被贬去惠州。七月，途中路过九江时，正好苏坚也在九江，两人得以重逢，而这阕《归朝欢》便是在这个时候创作的。整阕词虽有人生漂泊之感，但笔调雄健，气象宏阔，充满豪迈奋发的气概和积极开朗的情怀。

南乡子·重九涵辉楼呈徐君猷

苏轼

霜降水痕收。浅碧鳞鳞露远洲。酒力渐消风力软，飕飕（sōu）。破帽多情却恋头。

佳节若为酬。但把清樽断送秋。万事到头都是梦，休休。明日黄花蝶也愁。

Song of a Southern Country

To Governor Xu on Mountain-climbing Day

Su Shi

The tide flows out after the fall of frost,
From rippling green water a beach of sand will rise.
The soughing wind softens, the vigor of wine is lost,
When blows the breeze,
My sympathetic hat won't leave my head with ease.

How shall we pass the holiday?
Wine cup in hand, we may send autumn away
Everything will end in dreams,
It seems
Tomorrow fallen blooms will sadden butterflies.

深秋霜降时节，水位下降，波光粼粼处，江心的沙洲一不小心就露出头来。年岁渐长，酒力也慢慢减退了，微风刚一吹过，便觉得浑身都凉飕飕的，唯有头上的那顶破帽子，端的是自作多情，愣是不肯被风吹落。

这重阳佳节，究竟要如何应付过去？恐怕也只能借着这一盏清酒，一边打发时光，一边目送着秋天远去。世间万事，到头来，都是转瞬成空的梦境，所以就不要再提起那些兀自盘旋在风中的往事了。重阳节过后，五彩缤纷的菊花，便会逐渐失去往昔的鲜妍与妩媚，到那时，想必那些迷恋它们的蝴蝶，也都要陷入深深的愁绪之中了。

据弘治《黄州府志》记载，徐君猷任黄州知州时，“崇儒重道，下士爱民。苏东坡谪居黄州，与弟子由书云‘举目无亲，君猷一见如骨肉’”足见二人感情之深。

元丰五年（1082 年）的重阳节，当时词人被贬黄州，徐君猷为黄州知州。徐君猷没有因对方被贬而显出怠慢之意，与苏轼交情深厚。这阕《南乡子》即是词人在涵辉楼上写给徐君猷的一首怀人词。

南乡子·送述古

苏轼

回首乱山横，不见居人只见城。谁似临平山上塔，亭亭，迎客西来送客行。

归路晚风清，一枕初寒梦不成。今夜残灯斜照处，荧荧，秋雨晴时泪不晴。

Song of a Southern Country
Seeing Chen Shugu off

Su Shi

Turning my head, I find rugged mountains bar the sky,
I can no longer see you in the town.
Who can be like the hilltop tower looking down,
So high?
It welcomed you from the west and bids you goodbye.

I come back at dusk in a gentle breeze.
On chilly pillow how can I dream with ease?
Where will the flickering lamp shed its lonely light
Tonight?
When autumn rain no longer falls drop by drop,
Oh, will tears stop?

回头望去，远山横亘，乱石嶙峋，偌大的一座城池，只隐隐看到高大的城墙，却见不到哪怕一个百姓的踪影。故人终究还是离我远去，却叹谁能像那临平山上的高塔，总是笔直地矗立在山巅，日复一日地迎送着往来的过客？

回家的路上，晚风凄清，我满心都充斥着离别的惆怅。本以为会在梦中梦见故人，却不料晚寒彻骨，脑袋一挨上枕头就满腹凝愁，怎么也难以入眠。今夜里，残灯斜照，微光闪烁，四周一片昏暝暗淡，外面的秋雨虽然已经停歇了，但我思念故人的泪水却还挂在腮边，久久未尽。

宋神宗熙宁五年（1072 年），即苏轼赴杭州通判任的第二年，陈襄接替前任杭州太守沈立之职，成为苏轼的上司。熙宁七年（1074 年）七月，陈襄移任南都（今河南省商丘市南），苏轼追送其至临平（今浙江省杭州市余杭区），写下了这阕情真意切的送别词。

南宋文学家胡仔《苕溪渔隐丛话》后集卷三十八引《复斋漫录》：鲁直记江亭鬼所题词，有“泪眼不曾晴”之句。余以此鬼剽东坡乐章“秋雨晴时泪不晴”之语。

昭君怨·金山送柳子玉

苏轼

谁作桓(huán)伊三弄，惊破绿窗幽梦？新月与愁烟，满江天。

欲去又还不去，明日落花飞絮。飞絮送行舟，水东流。

The Lament of a Fair Lady
Farewell to Liu Ziyu on Mountain Jin

Su Shi

Who's playing on the flute a gloomy tune,
Breaking the green window's dreary dream?
The dreary mist veils the new moon,
Outspread in the sky over the stream.

You linger still though you must go.
Flowers and willow down will fall tomorrow.
They will see your boat off, laden with sorrow,
But still the stream will eastward flow.

夜深人静之际，不知道是谁吹响了一曲悠扬的笛韵，一下子便把人从幽深的好梦中惊醒。推开爬满藤蔓的窗户，但见一弯新月，正孤孤单单地挂在空荡荡的天上，远处，水天相接处，更是白茫茫一片，那缥缈迷蒙的烟雾，仿佛都被愁绪给填满了。

又到了说分别的时候，内心自是充满无尽惆怅，便兀自在想象中先预演了一番明天离别之际的情景。道了千万声珍重，送别的人儿，依旧呆呆地站立在江边，久久都不愿回去，那多情的落花柳絮，却像是明白他的心思一样，一路追逐着远去的行舟，默默代他送行。遗憾的是，滔滔的江水，竟全然不理会离人的心情，依旧奔流不息地向东流入大海，又哪里明白他内心的不舍与忧伤呢？

这阕词作于宋神宗熙宁七年（1074年）二月，是苏轼为送别柳子玉而作。柳子玉是润州丹徒（今江苏省镇江市丹徒区）人，与东坡谊兼戚友。熙宁六年（1073年）十一月，苏轼时任杭州通判，赴常州、润州一带赈饥，柳子玉亦起身欲赴舒州灵仙观，二人便结伴而行。次年二月，苏轼在金山（润州西北长江中）送别柳子玉，遂作此词以赠。

八声甘州·寄参寥子

苏轼

有情风万里卷潮来，无情送潮归。问钱塘江上，西兴浦口，几度斜晖？不用思量今古，俯仰昔人非。谁似东坡老，白首忘机。

记取西湖西畔，①正暮山好处，空翠烟霏。算诗人相得，如我与君稀。约它年、东还海道，愿谢公雅志莫相违。西州路，不应回首，为我沾衣。

①正暮一作：正春

Eight Beats of Ganzhou Song
For a Buddhist Friend

Su Shi

The heart-stirring breeze brings in the tidal bore;
The heartless wind sees it flow out from river shore.
At the river's mouth
Or the ferry south,
How many times have we heard parting chimes?
Don't grieve over the past!
The world changes fast.
Who could be like me,
Though white-haired, yet carefree?

Do not forsake the western shore of the lake:
On fine day the vernal hills are green;
On rainy day they are veiled by misty screen.
Few poets would be
Such bosom friends as you and me.
Do not forget in our old age,
We'll live together in hermitage.
Even if I should disappear,
You should not turn to weep for your compeer.

多情的风儿，从万里之外裹挟着潮水扑面而来，却又有谁知道，还是那无情的风儿，将那卷起千堆雪浪的潮水送归了它的老巢。我问你，是否还记得，在钱塘江上，还有那西兴渡口，我俩曾结伴共赏过几次夕阳斜晖？用不着仔细思量古往今来的种种变迁，俯仰之间，一切早已物是人非，谁能像我东坡苏老，白首之年，便即忘却了世俗的所有机诈之心？

记得，在西湖的西岸，春日里最美的山隈，峰峦叠翠，云烟缭绕，我和你一边饱览湖光山色，一边谈禅说道，好不恣意畅快。算起来，诗人中像我与你这样志趣相投又极为谈得来的朋友，实在稀微少见，也更显得弥足珍贵。

且约定好日后，你我要像东晋宰相谢安在复出后许下的承诺那样，毅然决然地沿着直通大海的长江航道，向东引退，回归潇洒，可千万别因为世俗的牵绊，违背了这一高雅的志向。当然，我也不会让你回首恸哭于西州路上，更不会让你为我被喷薄而出的泪水，无端地沾湿了衣襟。

参寥子，即僧人道潜，字参寥。精通佛典，工诗，以其精深的道义和清新的文笔，一直为苏轼所推崇，并与苏轼过从甚密，彼此结为莫逆之交。

苏轼贬谪黄州时，参寥不远千里赶去，追随他长达数年之久。元祐六年（1091 年），苏轼由杭州知州召为翰林学士承旨，将要离开杭州赴汴京时，作此词赠予参寥。

江城子·孤山竹阁送述古

苏轼

翠蛾羞黛怯人看。掩霜纨，泪偷弹。且尽一尊，收泪唱《阳关》。漫道帝城天样远，天易见，见君难。

画堂新构近孤山。曲栏干，为谁安？飞絮落花，春色属明年。欲棹小舟寻旧事，无处问，水连天。

Riverside Town

Farewell to Governor Chen at Bamboo Pavilion on Lonely Hill

Su Shi

Her eyebrows penciled dark, she feels shy to be seen.
Hidden behind a silken fan so green,
Stealthily she sheds tear on tear.
Let me drink farewell to you and hear
Her sing, with tears wiped away, her song of adieu.
Do not say the imperial town is as far as the sky.
It is easier to see the sun high
Than to meet you.

The newly built painted hall to Lonely Hill is near.
For whom is made
The winding balustrade?
Falling flowers and willow down fly;
Spring belongs to next year.
I try to row a boat to find the things gone by.
O whom can I ask? In my eye
I only see water one with the sky.

美人为即将而来的离别心痛难过，却又怕人看见她这副伤心模样，只好用手中的白纨扇轻轻遮挡住面部，偷偷地流下悲伤的泪水。

他就要走了，她唯一能做的，就是劝他尽情畅饮，不要再沉溺在这悲伤的情绪中无法自拔。收起婆娑的泪眼，她为他唱起了一支离别的《阳关曲》，却不料，悲从心中起，更惹她惆怅无限。都说那南都帝城比天还要遥远，可是天再远也容易见得，想要再见到他却是难上加难。

孤山上新建的画堂金碧辉煌、色彩斑斓，可他就要走了，那精巧玲珑的曲栏杆却是为了谁人安置，又有谁来陪她凭栏远眺西湖的殊胜风光？

放眼望去，落花与柳絮齐飞，看来想要与春色再度相逢，也只有等待来年了。怕只怕，明年的春日，当她撑着一叶小舟，沿着旧日的踪迹遍寻往日的清欢之际，那些陈年旧事，却是无法找人询问，触目所及之处，除了一片水天相连的茫茫水域，便是她缥缈若烟的心事。

这阕词，是苏轼在宋神宗熙宁七年（1074年），在杭州送别友人陈襄时，以歌伎的口吻，代她向陈襄表达惜别之意而作。

陈襄，字述古，其为杭州知州时，苏轼为通判，二人政治倾向基本相同，又是诗酒朋友，守杭期间甚为相得。这年七月，陈襄由杭州调知南都，僚友们为他举行了几次饯别宴会，而苏轼在这段时间更是为其先后写下了七首送别词，这阕《江城子》便是其中的一首。

永遇乐·长忆别时

苏轼

孙巨源以八月十五日离海州，坐别于景疏楼上。既而与余会于润州，至楚州乃别。余以十一月十五日至海州，与太守会于景疏楼上，作此词以寄巨源。

长忆别时，景疏楼上，明月如水。美酒清歌，留连不住，月随人千里。别来三度，孤光又满，冷落共谁同醉？卷珠帘、凄然顾影，共伊到明无寐。

今朝有客，来从濉（suī）上，能道使君深意。凭仗清淮，分明到海，中有相思泪。而今何在？西垣（yuán）清禁，夜永露华侵被。此时看、回廊晓月，也应暗记。

Joy of Eternal Union

Su Shi

I long remember when we bade goodbye
On Northeast Tower high,
The silvery moonlight looked like water bright.
But songs and wine, however fine,
Could not keep you from going away.
Only the moon followed you for miles on your way.
Since we parted, I've seen the moon wax and wane.
But who would drink with lonely me again?
Uprolling the screen,
Only my shadow's seen,
I stay awake until daybreak.

Today your friend comes from the river's end,
And brings to me your memory.
You ask the river clear
To bring nostalgic tear
As far as the east sea.
I do not know now where are you.
In palace hall by western wall,
Is your coverlet in deep night wet with dew?
When you see in the corridor the moving moon rays,
Could you forget the bygone days?

八月十五日孙巨源离开海州，在此之前他曾与诸位同僚在景疏楼上话别。不久他便与我在润州相聚，一路同行到楚州才分开。我于十一月十五日经过海州，与太守相会于景疏楼上，因想起孙巨源，便写了这阕词寄给他。

时常都会想起，你即将离开海州的时候，端坐在景疏楼上，与同僚们一起把盏欢饮的情景，窗外的月光就像水一般温柔清润。喝着美酒，唱着清歌，你流连忘返，自是快活得无以复加，只可惜，转身而去后，唯有一片痴诚的月光，跟随着你一同来到千里之外的汴京。

你走之后，到如今，正好三个月了，月亮也已经圆了三次。今天，又是一个月圆之夜，我一个人在客馆中喝着酒，凄凄冷冷清清，却有谁来与我同醉？无尽的寂寞中，我默默卷上珠帘，凄然地望了一眼窗外的月影，便这样和月光一起，相伴到天明，更是一宿无眠。

今天有个来自潍水旁的客人来见我，他告诉我，远方的你也很是想念我。你的相思泪，融入了清清的淮水，流进了奔腾不息的大海，可眼下，那个让我念了千遍万遍的你又在哪里呢？我知道，你在宫中禁苑值宿，而我却在担心，唯恐这漫漫长夜，露水会沾湿了你的被子。此时此刻，想必在回廊里抬头看着月亮的你，也应该正暗暗思慕着远方的我吧！

宋神宗熙宁七年（1074年）十一月十五日，苏轼在赴任密州太守的途中，经过海州（今江苏省连云港市）时，海州陈太守在景疏楼为其接风。而三个月前，苏轼的好友、原海州太守孙巨源离任时，亦曾在这里与群僚告别。十一月十五日，孙巨源已到汴京履新，任知制诰、起居舍人，在宫中办公，苏轼便于席上作此词寄之，以表思念之情。

虞美人·有美堂赠述古

苏轼

湖山信是东南美，一望弥千里。使君能得几回来？便使樽前醉倒更徘徊。

沙河塘里灯初上，水调谁家唱？夜阑风静欲归时，惟有一江明月碧琉璃。

The Beautiful Lady Yu
Written for Governor Chen at the Scenic Hall

Su Shi

How fair the lakes and hills of the Southern land are,
With plains extending wide and far!
How often, wine cup in hand, have you been here
That you can make us linger though drunk we appear!

By Sandy River Pool the new-lit lamps are bright.
Who is singing the water melody at night?
When I come back, the wind goes down, the bright moon paves
With emerald glass the river's waves.

登高远眺，千里美景尽收眼底，要说起这大千世界的湖光山色，还要数这里的最美。使君这一去，何时才能返回？请接着痛饮下几杯美酒吧，但愿这次醉倒后，就不用再起身离去了。

沙河塘华灯初放，车马水龙，好不热闹，却是谁在无尽的喧嚣声里，又弹唱起了那支动人心弦的水调歌？夜深了，风静了，当醉酒后的我们互相搀扶着准备回家之时，街上早已没了半个人影，唯有一轮明月，高高地挂在天边。再回首，钱塘江水在月光的映照下，更是澄澈得仿若一块绿色的琉璃，顷刻间，便让人忘却了一切的纷扰烦忧。

据《本事集》记载，熙宁七年（1074年）秋，苏轼任杭州通判时，杭州太守陈襄（字述古）即将罢任。陈襄离开杭州之前，曾宴客于有美堂，苏轼便即席赋写了此词。词中美好蕴藉的意象，是作者的感情与外界景物发生交流时形成的，亦是词人自我情感的象征，那千里湖山与一江明月，都是作者心灵深处缕缕情思的闪现。

更漏子·送孙巨源

苏轼

水涵空，山照市，西汉二疏乡里。
新白发，旧黄金，故人恩义深。
海东头，山尽处，自古空槎来去。
槎有信，赴秋期，使君行不归。

Song of Water Clock
Seeing Sun Juyuan Off

Su Shi

The water joins the sky,
The town girt with hills high,
This is a land of talents as of yore.
Your hair has turned white,
Of gold you make light,
You value friendship more.

East of the sea,
Where end the hills you see,
Boats come and go since days of old.
They have a date;
For you I'll wait.
Will you come back with the autumn cold?

海州城碧水连天，青山耸立，一派富丽堂皇的景象。这里是西汉时期疏广和疏受的故乡，叔侄二人，一为太傅，一为少傅，皆官居要职，却又同时请退乡里，历来深受世人景仰。为官海州数年，你又新添了白发，却博得州人殷勤相送，而这一切，都源于你给百姓们留下的深恩厚义啊！

大海的最东边，大山的尽头，自古以来，就传说有人从这里乘槎直抵天河。遗憾的是，客槎有来有往，每年的八月都会准时出现在海上，而你却未有归期，不免惹人惆怅无限。

此词为送别词，为宋神宗熙宁七年（1074年）十月，苏轼在楚州与孙洙（字巨源）分别时所作。

苏轼与孙洙，均与王安石政见不合，又有着共同的政治遭遇。为从政治斗争的旋涡中解脱出来，二人皆乞外任。此时，孙洙即将回朝任起居注、知制诰，很自然地，便引起了苏轼的思想波动，而这阕词便是在这种背景下创作而成。

阳关曲·中秋月

苏轼

暮云收尽溢清寒，银汉无声转玉盘。

此生此夜不长好，明月明年何处看。

Song of the Sunny Pass
The Mid Autumn Moon

Su Shi

Evening clouds withdrawn, pure cold air floods the sky;
The River of Stars mute, a jade plate turns on high.

How oft can we enjoy a fine mid-autumn night?
Where shall we view next year a silver moon so bright?

晚间的云雾全都被辽阔的苍穹收尽，周遭迅即溢出一抹舒爽的清寒。银河悄无声息地，缓缓转动着白玉圆盘，任月亮洒下无边的璀璨光华。

明月团团，兄弟团聚，想必今生再也不会遇见今夜这般的美好了，所以，切莫辜负了眼前的良辰美景。明年又会在什么地方观赏这一轮团团的明月呢，你我兄弟还能不能像现在这样依偎在一起把酒言欢呢？

创作完《水调歌头·明月几时有》之后不久，苏轼兄弟便得到了一次难得的团圆机会。

宋神宗熙宁九年（1076 年）冬，苏轼得到移知河中府的诏令，随即离开密州南下。次年春，苏辙自京师往迎，兄弟同赴开封，抵达陈桥驿之际，苏轼又奉命改知徐州，四月，苏辙随兄一起赴徐州任所，一直住到中秋以后方才离去。

七年来，兄弟俩第一次同赏月华，而不再是“千里共婵娟”。其时，苏辙有《水调歌头·徐州中秋》记其事，苏轼则写下这阕小词以为纪念，并题为“中秋月”。

千秋岁·苑边花外

黄庭坚

少游得谪，尝梦中作词云：『醉卧古藤阴下，了不知南北。』竟以元符庚辰，死于藤州光华亭上。崇宁甲申，庭坚窜宜州，道过衡阳。览其遗墨，始追和其《千秋岁》词。

苑边花外，记得同朝退。飞骑轧，鸣珂碎。齐歌云绕扇，赵舞风回带。严鼓断，杯盘狼藉犹相对。

洒泪谁能会？醉卧藤阴盖。人已去，词空在。兔园高宴悄，虎观英游改。重感慨，波涛万顷珠沉海。

A Thousand Years Old

Huang Tingjian

I remember after the court hours
We visited the garden of flowers.
Our horses ran,
Their gold bells rang.
Dancers with skirt in wind danced with their fan;
Into the cloud songstresses sang.
The drumbeats stopped when night was late;
We still sat face to face with leftovers in the plate.

Who understands why I shed tears after wine?
Drunk, we lay down in the shade of old vine.
Now you are gone, in vain
Your verses still remain.
In the garden of pleasure the feast is quiet;
In the Temple of White Tiger there's no more riot.
Deeply I sigh,
In the depth of the sea like a pearl you should lie.

秦少游被贬官后，曾在梦中作词：“醉卧古藤阴下，了不知南北。”没想到一语成谶，他竟于元符庚辰年死于藤州光华亭中。崇宁甲申年间，我被贬宜州，途中路过衡阳，看到秦观留下的遗作，才开始追和他的《千秋岁》一词。

还记得，在小园边的百花丛外，我们退朝后一起策马奔驰时的情景。那会儿的我们，是何等意气风发，马儿飞驰在大街上，只听得马头的玉饰被敲击得叮当作响，好不畅快。宴会上，我们征歌逐舞，一支齐地的歌曲，愣是唱得轻云绕扇；一段赵地的舞蹈，更是跳得风生水起，连腰带都不自觉地飘了起来。酒酣耳热之际，急促的鼓声突然停了下来，定睛望去，桌上的杯盘早已变得一片狼藉，而我们依然相对欢笑，乐不思归。

而今，就算挥洒下再多的泪水，也是阴阳相隔，我们又怎么能够再度相会呢？想你，念你，只能醉卧在如伞盖般的藤荫下默默思量，除此之外，别无他法。你早已离我而去，留下那么些华美的词作又有什么用呢？你不在了，一切皆成空，怎不惹人伤心难禁？

你走了，朝中华丽的宴会不复存在，宫廷里讲论经学之所的虎观，从今后也不会再出现我们这些才智杰出的人物了。你的逝去，让我感慨万千，而你就像万顷波涛中一颗璀璨的珍珠，彻底沉入了大海，再也无法找见。

黄庭坚和秦观都出自苏轼门下，宋哲宗元祐年间，又同在朝堂为官。其时，黄庭坚任《神宗实录》检讨官，秦观则为秘书省正字兼国史院编修官，二人意气相投，关系紧密。

据词的序文，可知该词作于宋徽宗崇宁三年（1104年）。当时黄庭坚被贬宜州，经过衡阳时，在秦观生前好友、衡州知州孔毅甫处，见到了他的遗作《千秋岁》词。宋哲宗元符三年（1100年），秦观在贬谪途中逝于藤州，而黄庭坚追和《千秋岁》词之际，距离秦观之死已有四年之久。

虞美人·大光祖席，醉中赋长短句

陈与义

张帆欲去仍搔首，更醉君家酒。吟诗日日待春风，及至桃花开后却匆匆。

歌声频为行人咽，记著樽前雪。明朝酒醒大江流，满载一船离恨向衡州。

The Beautiful Lady Yu
Written while Drunk in a Farewell Feast

Chen Yuyi

Setting sail, I will go but still I scratch my hair,
Drunk with your wine and care.
We've waited for spring breeze, crooning verse day by day,
But when peach blossoms blow, in haste I'll go away.

The songstress sobs when I'm about to go.
Can I forget, wine cup in hand, her song of snow?
When I awake tomorrow, the river still flows;
Laden with parting grief, the ship still southward goes.

远去的船帆都张挂起来了，我却挠着头不忍离去，只一杯接着一杯地畅饮着你为我送行的美酒。我们曾终日里依伴在一起吟诗赏景，期待着春天的到来，没想到等桃花开了，却又不得不匆匆地告别。

就连告别宴会上的歌伎，都为我们的离情别绪所感动，歌声几度呜咽，更惹我几度惆怅莫名。我不仅要记住这位歌伎，也要记住这次饯别和你对我的情意。或许，等到明朝酒醒之后，此身已随船驶入湘江，而那船儿亦已载着满舱的离恨，一路把我送向衡州。

宋高宗建炎三年（1129 年），陈与义与友人席益（字大光）在衡山相遇。当时，陈与义因躲避金兵而抵达湖南，而席益则卸掉官职在衡山一带流浪。二人相聚后不久，陈与义便又离开衡山，在席益为他举办的饯别宴上写下了这阕《虞美人》词，以别友人。

陈与义（1090 年—1139 年），字去非，号简斋。其先祖居京兆（今陕西省西安市），自曾祖陈希亮从眉州迁居洛阳后，故为洛阳（今河南省洛阳市）人，是北宋末、南宋初的杰出诗人。

诗尊杜甫，前期清新明快，后期雄浑沉郁；同时也工于填词，其词存于今者虽仅十余首，但却别具风格，豪放处尤近于苏轼，语意超绝，笔力横空，疏朗明快，自然浑成，著有《简斋集》。

虞美人·扁舟三日秋塘路

陈与义

余甲寅岁自春官出守湖州。秋杪，道中荷花无复存者。乙卯岁，自琐闼以病得请奉祠，卜居青墩镇。立秋后三日行。舟之前后如朝霞相映，望之不断也。以长短句记之。

扁舟三日秋塘路，平度荷花去。病夫因病得来游，更值满川微雨洗新秋。

去年长恨拿舟晚，空见残荷满。今年何以报君恩，一路繁花相送到青墩。

The Beautiful Lady Yu

Chen Yuyi

Three days after the Autumn Day
My boat goes along the lotus poolside way
Ill, I come for an autumn view;
The drizzling rain has washed clear autumn new.

Last year's regret of coming late would still remain;
I saw but withered blooms in vain.
How should I show my gratitude this year,
When all the way flowers in bloom appear?

我曾在绍兴四年（1134年）出守湖州时路过这里，时已秋深，道中荷花已一朵不存。到了次年，我因病得请奉祠，卜居青墩，在立秋后三日启程，又从这里经过，但见满湖荷花盛开，舟前舟后，仿佛朝霞相映，一眼望不到边际，遂记之以词。

划着小舟在秋日的荷塘上行驶了三天，船儿在波光潋滟的水面上平稳地行进着，船舷两侧的荷花纷纷向后退去，恍临仙境。我因为托病离开了朝堂，才有机会来此一游，又恰好遇上雨后一碧如洗的秋山，心情自是畅快得无以复加。

遗憾的是，去年行舟出来游玩时已经太晚，放眼望去，只看见满塘残败的荷花，无甚了了。今年我该拿什么来报答君主的恩情呢？如果没有他的许诺，我又如何能够带着这无比欢快的心情，任满塘繁盛的花儿一路把我送到青墩呢？

宋高宗绍兴五年（1135年）六月，词人托病辞职，以显谟阁直学士提举江州太平观，实际上则是领俸禄闲居，卜居青墩，并于立秋后三日出发。这阕词可能作于船上，或词人抵达青墩后不久的日子里。

第六章

远山×沧海

CHAPTER SIX

Far-off hills and vast sea

忆秦娥·梅谢了

刘克庄

梅谢了，塞垣冻解鸿归早。鸿归早，

凭伊问讯，大梁遗老。

浙河西面边声悄，淮河北去炊烟少。

炊烟少。宣和宫殿，冷烟衰草。

Dream of a Fair Maiden

Liu Kezhuang

Mume blossoms fail,
Ice melts on the frontier where early go wild geese.
Early going wild geese,
Would you ask, please,
After old folks in ancient capital?

On western frontier we hear no war cries;
On northern river we see less chimney smoke rise.
Seeing chimney smoke rise,
In ancient palace hall, alas!
There're but cold smoke and withered grass.

枝头的梅花渐渐地凋谢了，北方边塞的冰雪也跟着融化了，那些振翅高飞的大雁，更是早早地向北飞去了。早早归去的鸿雁啊，就请你们代表我，衷心地问候下故都的家乡父老吧！

浙江西面，镇江一带，地处边防要塞，却始终疏于防守，竟然听不到一点兵戈之声。淮河以北，是金国占领的沦陷区，人烟稀少，一片荒芜。曾经繁华奢靡的东京城，即便是宋徽宗居住过的宫殿，也早就荒草遍地，尘烟缭绕。

宋宁宗开禧二年（1206年），韩侂胄仓促的北伐失败了。和议之后，昏庸的皇帝和掌权的投降派大臣立马就把恢复中原的大业置之脑后。然而，大宋的爱国志士们并没有忘记失陷的国土，他们日日为国家的前途担忧，词人也正是在这种心境下，满怀忧虑和期望地写下了这阕词。

刘克庄（1187年—1269年），初名灼，字潜夫，号后村，福建莆田（今福建省莆田市）人。南宋诗人、词人、诗论家，是宋末文坛的领袖，也是辛派词人的重要代表作家，多词风豪迈慷慨之作。在江湖派诗人中年寿最长，官位最高，成就也最大，晚年则致力于辞赋创作，并提出了很多革新理论。

六州歌头·项羽庙

李冠

秦亡草昧，刘项起吞并。鞭寰huán宇。驱龙虎。扫欃chán枪。斩长鲸。血染中原战。视余耳，皆鹰犬。平祸乱。归炎汉。势奔倾。兵散月明。风急旌旗乱，刁斗三更。共虞姬相对，泣听楚歌声。玉帐魂惊。泪盈盈。念花无主。凝愁苦。挥雪刃，掩泉扃jiōng。时不利。骓zhuī不逝。闲阴陵。叱chì追兵。鸣咽摧天地，望归路，忍偷生。功盖世，何处见遗灵。江静水寒烟冷，波纹细、古木凋零。遣行人到此，追念益伤情。胜负难凭。

Prelude to the Song of Six States
The Temple of Xiang Yu
Li Guan

At the Qin's close
Liu and Xiang rose.
Whipping the world driving dragons and tigers away,
Killing the whales and sweeping the comets in array.
Beating the foe,
Quelling the woe,
Liu won the war
With an uproar.
Xiang's army dispersed in moonlight,
His flags pellmell at the dead of night.
He listened in the tent for long
His native Southern song
With Lady Yu in tears,
Her jade-like soul in fears.

The beauty grieved to lose her lord;
She killed herself with snow-bright sword.
Unfortunately he could not run his horse;
Surrounded he could still frighten the pursuing force.
Could sky and earth not be moved to tears?
Gazing on homeward way ahead,
Could he survive the dead?
Heroism unsurpassed
O where to find the hero's soul at last?
The river's still, the mist and water freeze,
It ripples in the breeze
Before the withered ancient trees.
Visitors would be moved none the less.
Could a hero be judged by failure or success?

秦朝亡于混乱黑暗的政治后，天下便成了刘邦和项羽逐鹿的战场。这项羽年轻有为，欲以一己之力征服天下，以成就霸王之业。他有着龙虎一样彪悍的战将供他驱使，在巨鹿之战中，他俘虏了秦国大将王离，招降了主帅章邯，彻底消灭了秦军主力。

然而，在和刘邦血战中原的交锋中，他的部将陈余被杀，张耳投降，一个个的，皆被刘邦视作了鹰犬。最后，刘邦取得了决定性的胜利，各路诸侯先后归附于大汉，项羽则由强转弱，陷入困境，无奈之下，只好率众南走。

垓下之围中，士气低落的楚军，于月明之夜迅即土崩瓦解，四下溃散。大风刮倒了旌旗，三更半夜里，项羽惊闻帐外楚歌四起，心知大势已去，却只能与爱妾虞姬相对而坐，流着眼泪一起在熟悉的乡音里诀别。

英雄末路，望着爱姬泪眼婆娑的面庞，项羽的心痛到了极点。如果他就这么死了，虞姬以后的生活该怎么办呢？他无法想象，失去了他的虞姬会遭遇怎样的结局，疲惫的脸上爬满了愁容。还能怎么办呢？虞姬为表心志，毅然决然地当着他的面挥刀自刎，他亦只能和着两行热泪，把她草草葬在了水边。

时运不济，唯有乌骓宝马还陪伴在他身侧。突出重围后的项羽，先是被困于阴陵，继而又被追兵追至乌江畔，真正是穷途末路，无计可施。放眼望去，天昏地暗，家乡的方向依然有着他无限的牵挂，可他却不愿意忍辱偷生，以一个失败者的身份回归江东，最终选择了和虞姬一样的结局，手起刀落，一命呜呼。

他功高盖世，是一个顶天立地的大英雄。遗憾的是，时过境迁，却不知道该去哪里找寻他的遗灵。烟波浩渺的乌江水澄静依旧，浪寒烟冷，早已不见了当年的金戈铁马，唯余粼粼的波纹，还有些许稀疏凋零的古木，在历史的尘埃里缅怀过往。

俱往矣，一切的一切皆成过眼云烟，而今，若有行人探古至此，想必在追怀项羽的同时，也会和我一样，对他怀着无尽的同情和深深的哀悼，更不会以成败论英雄，抹杀他曾经的卓越功劳。

这是一阕咏史怀古词。全词通篇檃栝《史记》中的《项羽本纪》，不仅把项羽从起兵到失败的曲折历程一一熔铸于词中，更将项羽的英雄气概表现得一览无余。

李冠，字世英，齐州历城（今山东省济南市）人。生卒年均不详，约宋真宗天禧中前后在世。与王樵、贾同齐名，又与刘潜同时以文学称于京东。

举进士不第，得同三礼出身，调乾宁主簿。著有《东皋集》二十卷，不传。存词五首。沈谦《填词杂说》赞其《蝶恋花》，“数点雨声风约住，朦胧淡月云来去”句，以为“‘红杏枝头春意闹’‘云破月来花弄影’俱不及”。

将进酒·城下路

贺铸

城下路，凄风露，今人犁田古人墓。岸头沙，带蒹葭，漫漫昔时流水今人家。黄埃赤日长安道，倦客无浆马无草。开函关，掩函关，千古如何不见一人闲？六国扰，三秦扫，初谓商山遗四老。驰单车，致缄jiān书，裂荷焚芰jì接武曳长裾。高流端得酒中趣，深入醉乡安稳处。生忘形，死忘名。谁论二豪初不数刘伶？

Invitation to Wine

He Zhu

The wind and dew so drear
Bring the buried no cheer.
We till the ground where were the graves of olden days.
Reed and rush grow
By rivershore,
Houses are built where flowed rivers of yore.
Yellow dust is raised under the sun on the way
To the capital town.
Tired wayfarers have no drink and horses no hay.
The passage closed down
Opens again;
As of old we see but passengers come and go.

Six States no more. began Qin's reign.
Where are the loyal hermits then?
Driving cabs on the way
And sending letters away,
They burned old things and put on robes in display.
Wise men enjoy delight in wine;
Drunk, they will find the country fine.
Neglecting health
And fame and wealth,
Why should I care for what the lords and hermits say?

城下的道路，裹着凄冷的风露，今人耕种的田地，竟是古人的坟墓。岸边滩头的白沙，连接着成片的蒹葭，昔日的江河流水都变成了而今的陆地，住满了村户人家。

通往长安的大道，黄沙滚滚，烈日炎炎，疲倦的过客，找不到可以饮用的水，更找不见可以给马喂食的料草。天下之事，总是太平了又变乱，函谷关一会儿打开一会儿闭关，周而复始，无限循环，千百年来，怎么就见不到一个悠闲自得的人？

秦末之季，群雄纷争，六国争权，汉高祖刘邦一马当先，横扫天下，愣是建立了千古不朽的基业。本以为世风转好，才出了那隐居深山、不慕荣华的“商山四皓”，谁知道吕后只是派了一介使臣，送了一封书信，他们就彻底撕下伪装，忙不迭地应声出山，住到了富丽堂皇的侯门中。

既然做不了隐士，那就沉入醉乡做个酒徒吧！只有高人名士，才能真正领会到酒的情趣，才能体会到醉后沉入梦乡睡个安稳觉的美好滋味。活着的时候放浪不羁，死后亦无须留名，谁说那贵介公子、缙绅处士，就胜过潇洒落拓、嗜酒如命的刘伶？

贺铸生活在北宋晚期，史书称他喜谈天下事，但其担任的一直都是些难以施展抱负的文武小职，心中难免郁闷，而这些在他的词作中也多有反映。此词调寄《小梅花》，“将进酒”实即词题，它原系乐府诗题，多写志士失路的悲愤，然自《花间集》以来，文人所作，以歌筵酒席浅斟低唱者为多，而用以书愤且得乐府诗遗意的，在词坛中还是比较新颖的。

贺铸（1052年—1125年），字方回，又名贺三愁，人称贺梅子。卫州（今河南省卫辉市）人。北宋词人。

凌歊·铜人捧露盘引

贺铸

控沧江，排青嶂，燕台凉。驻彩仗、乐未渠央。岩花蹬(dēng)蔓，妒千门、珠翠倚新妆。舞闲歌悄，恨风流、不管余香。

繁华梦，惊俄顷，佳丽地，指苍茫。寄一笑、何与兴亡！量船载酒，赖使君、相对两胡床。缓调清管，更为侬、三弄斜阳。

Scraping the Sky
Song of the Yellow Mountains

He Zhu

The reinless stream goes through
The steep cliff blue
Under the Peak scraping the sky.
Colored flags flew,
The king made merry far and nigh.
Flowers and vine
Would envy ladies' attire so fine.
Nor dance nor song,
However gallant, could last long.

The splendid dream
Soon fades away,
Fair land and stream
Turn pale and grey.
I see in laughter
The rise and fall before and after.
I'd sail with wine.
You in your place and I in mine.
Playing on the flute, will you
Sing for me to the setting sun adieu?

长江流至当涂以后，因两岸山势陡峭，江面变得狭窄，形成天门、牛渚两处极为险要的江防重地，形同锁钥。水流湍急，仿若推开青山顺流而下，自是气象万千。

宋孝武帝曾经登临的凌歊台依旧还在，却早已失去了当日的风流绮丽。想当年，彩色的仪仗队伍立满了山头，欢声笑语响彻云霄，但即便如此，帝王将相们还是觉得没有尽兴。

随行的妃嫔宫娥，个个盛妆靓饰，环佩叮当，千娇百媚，就连山花藤蔓都因自惭形秽而产生了妒意。俱往矣，喧闹的场面，到如今早已烟消云散，再也没有什么轻歌曼舞，无限风流。只余一个缥缈的恨字，又哪里管得了那些野花野草呢？

繁华恰似一场春梦，转瞬便即成空。曾经的秀丽江山，现如今，不管伸手指向哪里，都是一片荒芜苍茫。还能怎么样呢？昔日请长缨、系天骄的雄心壮志，已经被一点一点地消磨殆尽，也只好把这千古兴亡事且付之一笑罢了。

量船载酒，继续徜徉在山水之间，所幸还有使君陪我一起坐在折叠椅上相对而望，可以稍稍慰我旅途寂寞。夕阳西下，百无聊赖，只好请你再为我吹奏三支笛曲，切莫辜负了这大好的黄昏。

这是一阕登临怀古之作。贺铸约于宋徽宗崇宁四年（1105年）至大观二年（1108年）通判太平州，这阕词当作于这段时间内。

463年，南朝宋孝武帝刘骏南游，登凌歊台，并建避暑离宫；六百余年后，贺铸亦到此处，观旧址，叹时世变迁，人生苦短，遂作此词。

台城游·南国本潇洒

贺铸

南国本潇洒，六代浸豪奢。台城游冶，襞(bì)笺能赋属宫娃。云观登临清夏，璧月流连长夜，吟醉送年华。回首飞鸳瓦，却羡井中蛙。

访乌衣，成白社，不容车。旧时王谢、堂前双燕过谁家？楼外河横斗挂，淮上潮平霜下，樯影落寒沙。商女篷窗罅(xià)，犹唱后庭花！

The Terrace Wall

He Zhu

Gallant the Southern land far and wide,
Six Dynasties in opulence vied.
Wine, woman and song on Terrace Wall,
Eight beauties wrote verse in palace hall.
In summer clear they mounted the cloud-scraping height,
Under the jadelike moon they loitered in long night,
They drank and crooned the years away.
Leaving the lovebirds tiles pell-mell
They tried to hide like frogs in a well.

On street of mansions overgrown with grass
No cabs could pass.
The swallows in the mansions of bygone days,
In whose hall now do they stay?
Over the tower the Silver River bars the sky,
The Plough hangs high.
The tide runs up and down on frosty River Huai.
The shadow of townwalls on cold sand falls.
Through the window gap of the bower
I see the songstress sing the Backyard Flower.

南国金陵本是一个景色宜人的好去处，六朝金粉，豪奢无度，却改变不了王朝接连更替的命运。那会儿的贵族们生活骄奢淫逸，时常在台城举行各种各样的游乐活动，宫中的美人们都能在彩笺上作诗，以为助兴。

清朗宁和的初夏，帝王后妃们登上高耸入云的楼台寻欢作乐，好不恣意。白玉璧一样圆润的月亮高高地挂在天边，流连了一整个夜晚，贵人们则忙着在月华下吟诗品酒，借以打发这许多无聊的时光。

回首往事，金碧辉煌的陈朝宫殿，转瞬间，就被绵延的战火焚毁，那陈国的君主陈叔宝却携着他最心爱的妃子躲进了井中，狼狈不堪。唉，往事随风而去，真正值得人们钦羡的却是那井中之蛙，即便遭遇亡国之恨，又哪里会遭受陈后主那样的屈辱呢？

寻访昔日繁华富庶的乌衣巷，而今的它却从过去贵族的聚集地，沦落成了脏乱的贫民窟，道窄得竟连马车都过不去。曾经翩跹着飞过王、谢两大家族堂前的那对燕子，眼下又飞落到谁家了呢？

秋高气爽，夜深人静，登楼望远，但见星光闪耀的银河，自东南至西北横斜于天，北斗斜挂若垂，轻柔的月光梦幻般地笼罩着水流平缓的秦淮河，把几桅樯影清晰地映照在铺满银霜的寒沙之上。

倾耳，有歌女的歌声，正透过舟船的缝隙，断断续续地随风传来，如泣如诉，如梦如幻，依然还是那曲不知亡国之恨的《玉树后庭花》，听来更惹人无限神伤。

这阕词作于宋哲宗元祐三年至五年（1088 年—1090 年）间。当时贺铸正在历阳石碛戍任管界巡检（负责地方上训治甲兵、巡逻州邑，捕捉盗贼等的武官），只不过是一个供人驱遣的武弁而已。他空怀壮志，报国无门，只能把自己吊古伤今、抑塞磊落之情，一一融入历史的反思和凄清冷寂的画面之中，读来发人深省。

六州歌头·少年侠气

贺铸

少年侠气，交结五都雄。肝胆洞，毛发耸。立谈中，死生同。一诺千金重。

推翘勇，矜豪纵。轻盖拥，联飞鞚(kòng)，斗城东。轰饮酒垆(lú)，春色浮寒瓮(wèng)，吸海垂虹。①闲呼鹰嗾(sǒu)犬，白羽摘雕弓，狡穴俄空。乐匆匆。

似黄粱梦，辞丹凤，明月共，漾孤篷。官冗从，怀倥(kǒng)偬(zǒng)；落尘笼，簿书丛。鹖(hé)弁(biàn)如云众，供粗用，忽奇功。笳鼓动，渔阳弄，思悲翁。不请长缨，系取天骄种，剑吼西风。恨登山临水，手寄七弦桐，目送归鸿。

①闲呼一作：间呼

Prelude to the Song of Six States
He Zhu

A gallant young man calls
For heroes from five capitals.
He would see through heart and soul true.
While talking in wrath, his hair
Would stand on end, he'd share
The fate of life and death with friends bold,
And keep his word as dear as gold.
They vie in bravery and gallantry.
In eastern town they go in carriage light
And ride on horse side by side as if in flight.
They drink and bring to the jar cold
The hue of spring as rainbow on the sea.
Their eagles and dogs pursue their preys which flee.
They bend their bows and shoot arrows of feathers white.
Leaving the empty cave,
They are so brave.

Since I left the capital town,
Life has passed like a dream with ups and downs.
I sail a boat alone,
Accompanied but by the moon.
A petty officer like me,
How can I wish to kill the foe?
Fallen in dusty world, can I be free from woe?
The officers in crowd
Only follow like cloud
How can they ride their steeds and do great deeds?
Heating the horn and drumbeats,
How can I do in war great feats?
I can't bind with a long rope the proud enemy,
Leaving my sword in vain sigh,
I will not climb the mountain high,
But play my lute of seven strings in western breeze,
And gaze on flying wild geese.

少年多侠气，喜欢结交各地的英雄豪杰。我们意气相投，肝胆相照，三言两语，即成生死之交；我们心无城府，义薄云天，在邪恶势力面前，敢于裂眦耸发，无所畏惧；我们重义轻财，一诺千金；我们推崇勇敢，以豪侠纵气为尚。

我们时常驾着轻车，骑着骏马，结伴出现在东京城的大街小巷。我们时常轰笑着聚集在酒店里豪饮，每次都迫不及待地打开酒坛，像海面上垂下的长虹一样，大口大口地喝着美酒，顷刻间便喝得天昏地暗。间或还会带着鹰犬去城外打猎，当我们张弓射出羽箭之际，各种野兽的巢穴，瞬间便会被搜罗一空。遗憾的是，时光荏苒，欢乐总是太匆匆，现如今却是再也找不见当初那样的喜悦与明媚了。

短暂的欢愉，就像卢生的黄粱梦一样，是那么不真切、不长久。很快，我就离开京城了，终日驾着孤舟流浪在迁徙的路上，唯有一轮明月相伴。岁月倥偬，官职低微的我，就像一只落入囚笼的雄鹰，每天只能伏案做些琐碎而又烦冗的文书工作，更不要说保家卫国、建立奇功了。

像我这样郁郁不得志、终日一筹莫展的武官，多得犹如天边集聚的云彩，却都被支派到地方上去打杂，劳碌于文书案牍，不能杀敌疆场、建功立业。笳鼓敲响了，边境又乱起来了，战争眼看着就要爆发了，想我这悲愤的老兵却是无路请缨，不能为国御敌，生擒西夏酋帅，就连随身佩带的宝剑都在秋风中发出了愤怒的吼声，不断为我叫屈。无奈之下，我只能怀着满腔的怅恨，继续登山游水，目送头顶的大雁翩跹着归去，将忧思都寄予指间的琴弦。

这阕词作于宋哲宗元祐三年（1088年）秋。时西夏屡犯边界，贺铸在和州（今安徽省和县一带）任管界巡检，尽管官卑人微，却始终关心着国家大事。眼看宋王朝政治日益混乱，词人虽义愤填膺，却又无力上达，于是挥笔写下了这篇豪放名作。

行路难·缚虎手

贺铸

缚虎手，悬河口，车如鸡栖马如狗。白纶巾，扑黄尘，不知我辈可是蓬蒿人？衰兰送客咸阳道，天若有情天亦老。作雷颠，不论钱，谁问旗亭美酒斗十千？酌大斗，更为寿，青鬓长青古无有。笑嫣然，舞翩然，当垆秦女十五语如弦。遗音能记秋风曲，事去千年犹恨促。揽流光，系扶桑，争奈愁来一日却为长。

Hard Is the Way

He Zhu

Binding a tiger with bare hands,
Speaking as flowing water expands,
I ride in a cagelike cab, on a doglike steed.
Putting on silk hood white,
Raising yellow dust light,
Who knows we countrymen can do great deed?
The withered orchids see me off on homeward way,
If heaven had a heart, he would grow old today.
I'd play a madman old
And would not care for gold.
I'd spend ten thousand coins to buy good wine
And write in high pavilion verses fine.

Let's fill our brimful cup,
To old age let's live up!
No man can grow old with black hair since days of yore.
A smiling face
Dances with grace,
The western songstress at fifteen would speak and sing
As a musical string.
She sings the song of autumn breeze,
Which, sung long ago, could still please.
A thousand years have passed like one day and no more.
Stop time that flies
Ant bind sunrise!
But when sorrow comes near,
One day seems as long as a year.

能够徒手搏猛虎者是为勇士，口若悬河的辩者是为谋士，倘若逢时，这样的文武奇才当高车驷马，上黄金台，封万户侯。可怜眼下的我，穷困潦倒，乘坐的车若鸡舍般局促，骑的马也跟狗一样瘦小。头戴着平民百姓的白丝巾，京城的沙尘追着飞马扑面席卷而来，却不知道此次进京，是否可以像李白一样取得富贵。

遗憾的是我生不逢时，终究还是狼狈不堪地离开了京城，唯有路边渐渐枯萎的兰花，目送着我无助地走在凄凉的官道上。假若上天是有情意的，也一定会因为同情我的遭遇而悲伤得慢慢老去吧？即便如此，我也要效仿古代的侠士雷颠，做了好事不受酬金，但一旦遇到好酒，哪怕它价值万钱，也要喝到一醉方休才行。

我要痛快淋漓地倾倒酒坛，喝光所有的美酒，祝福我长命百岁、身体健康、鬓发长青，古所未有。叹，人生苦短，当及时行乐，你看那当垆卖酒的秦地女子，巧笑嫣然，起舞翩跹，刚刚年届十五，花般的年纪，说起话来，仿若琵琶上弹奏出的弦音一样动听，尔后的日子就要过得这般无忧无虑才有意思。

汉武帝留传于世的遗音绝响《秋风辞》，虽历经千年的岁月变迁，至今仍让人记忆犹新，每每听来，都不由得让人恼恨起这人生太过短促。多想抓住这流逝的光阴永远都不撒手啊，多想把太阳永远都拴在扶桑树上不让它落下西山啊，却无奈，当忧愁阵阵袭来的时候，倒又觉得这日子一天更比一天长，终是度日如年，煎熬难耐。

贺铸文武兼备，性格耿直，深具英雄气概，虽出身尊贵，却因始终得不到朝廷重用，导致雄才大略无法实现，终生失意不遇，积累了满腹的牢骚，这阕词便抒写了他报国无门、功业难成的失意情怀。全词采用刚健的笔调、高亢的声调写成，章法上极尽抑扬顿挫之能事，行文上跌宕生姿，属于贺词中的幽洁悲壮之作，在北宋词坛上也是非常突出的佳作。

八声甘州·寿阳楼八公山作

叶梦得

故都迷岸草，望长淮、依然绕孤城。想乌衣年少，芝兰秀发，戈戟(jǐ)云横。坐看骄兵南渡，沸浪骇奔鲸。转盼东流水，一顾功成。

千载八公山下，尚断崖草木，遥拥峥嵘。漫云涛吞吐，无处问豪英。信劳生、空成今古，笑我来、何事怆遗情。东山老，可堪岁晚，独听桓筝。

Eight Beats of Ganzhou Song
Ancient Battlefield
Ye Mengde

The shore of the ancient capital in rank grass drowned,
The River Huai still goes around
The lonely ancient battleground.
The black-gowned young heroes like orchid bright
Wielded their spears to bar the cloud.
They beat the hostile army proud
Crossing the River Long
Like surging waves to frighten away the whale strong.
O how I wish the river which eastward flows
Would turn back to beat the foes!

A thousand years have passed,
At the foot of the mountain grass grows thick and fast,
The broken cliffs remember still the glory past.
Though clouds break on high and waves surge below,
Where to find heroes of so long ago?
All labor lost now as then will pass away
Why should I come to grieve over the bygone day!
In Eastern Hills the hero's old.
Could he alone in his late years hear the lute cold?

放眼望去，淮河依旧环绕着楚都寿春这座孤城，到处都是丛生的野草、迷蒙的烟霭。想当年，在淝水之战中大破苻坚军队的前锋都督谢玄，正年轻有为，意气风发，统领数万精兵，有着非同一般的雄才大略。

他以逸待劳，坐看骄兵渡河南来，以出其不意之势，迎头痛击，那号称有百万之众的前秦军队，瞬间便如同受惊的巨鲸，在淝水中溃奔而逃。就这样，顾盼之间，谢玄便建立了不朽的功业，他的名字亦注定会永远被载入史册，成为后来者学习的榜样。

千载之后，八公山的草木一如当年，纷纷簇拥着险峻的峰峦，山头的云涛聚了又散，昔日的豪杰却杳无踪迹。谢氏子弟劳累了一生，他们建立的功业，都已随着岁月的流逝而慢慢消殒，只留下一座孤城，伴着八公山和山下的流水，依旧不停地向人们诉说着当年的英雄气概。

世事恍如春梦，可笑我太过执着，吊古伤今又何必沉溺其中？可叹谢家子弟的主心骨谢安，却在晚年的时候遭到孝武帝的疏远，只能和着一怀寂寞，独听名士桓伊为他弹响一支筝曲，黯然神伤。

这阕词于宋高宗绍兴三年（1133年）前后，词人登寿阳（今安徽省寿县）城楼及八公山时有感而作。叶梦得在寿阳八公山登高望远，想到谢家子弟大败前秦军队的故事，遂引发思古之幽情，在缅怀谢安、谢玄等人的千秋功业之际，更自伤年暮岁晚、一事无成，遂写下了这篇词作。

叶梦得（1077年—1148年），字少蕴，号肖翁、石林居士。原籍吴县（今江苏省苏州市），居住乌程（今浙江省湖州市）。绍圣四年（1097年）登进士第，历任翰林学士、户部尚书、江东安抚大使等官职，死后追赠检校少保。晚年隐居湖州弁山玲珑山石林，所著诗文多以石林为名，如《石林燕语》《石林词》《石林诗话》等。

在北宋末年到南宋前半期的词风变异过程中，叶梦得是起到先导和枢纽作用的重要词人之一。作为南渡词人中年辈较长的一位，叶梦得开拓了南宋前半期以“气”入词的词坛新路，而他的“气”，则主要表现在英雄气、狂气和逸气三个方面。

念奴娇·云峰横起

叶梦得

云峰横起，障吴关三面，真成尤物。倒卷回潮目尽处，秋水黏天无壁。绿鬓人归，如今虽在，空有千茎雪。追寻如梦，漫余诗句犹杰。

闻道尊酒登临，孙郎终古恨，长歌时发。万里云屯瓜步晚，落日旌旗明灭。鼓吹风高，画船遥想，一笑吞穷发。当时曾照，更谁重问山月。

Charm of a Maiden Singer

Ye Mengde

Cloudy peaks bar the sky,
Screening three sides of Kingdom Wu,
A marvel on high.
The tide flows out as far as I stretch my eye,
The autumn water like a wall blends with the blue.
I left the town with black hair; now I come again
With a thousand stems of snow-white hair in vain.
The past gone like a dream,
My verse would pour out as a stream.

'T is said young General Sun oft came here with wine
And crooned verse fine.
To our regret early he died.
Clouds spread for miles and miles over the riverside;
The setting sun cast light and shade on Melon Isle.
With the drumbeats the wind runs high;
In my painted boat my thoughts fly.
When can we beat the foe with smiles?
The moon has shone on heroes of yore,
But who would care for heroes any more?

云雾缭绕的山峰，仿若屏障一样，把古吴国所属地区遮去了三面，真是尤异奇特。

从江干极目远眺，那回潮倒卷之处，秋水与长天浑然一体，根本就没法找到它的边际。

第一次来建康的时候，我不过才五十出头，还不算老，离开之际，尚有满头青丝，而这次重返故地，人虽然还算康健，却已是满头白发、年过花甲的老人了。人生苦短，所有的追寻都恰似一场幻梦，到如今，精力已大不如前，唯有诗情未减，下笔仍若往日那般雄浑奔放。

蓦然回首，又想起东汉末年崛起江东的孙策，他时常携酒登临北固山游宴，引吭高歌，英姿勃发，豪气干云。当年的孙策正值英年，手握雄兵，有着澄清寰宇的伟大志向，只可惜他壮志未酬身先死，唯留下不尽的遗恨，供后人默默咀嚼。

兴尽而归，坐在船上向西望去，万里浓云绵亘，北岸临江的瓜步一带，军营中的旌旗，在落日余晖的映照下，时而明丽，时而黯淡。鼓角声漫随秋风从远处缓缓飘来，身在画船中的我，又忍不住胡思乱想起来。淮水以北的地区已被金兵占领，大宋政权岌岌可危，收复失地渺不可期，究竟什么时候，王师才能北定中原，深入金国腹地，直捣黄龙府，以实现举国父老的愿望？

月亮从东山升起来了，就是这个月亮，曾照遍古往今来的人儿，其中既有孙策，也有率军南下进驻瓜步的北魏太武帝，当年的情景，它通通可以做证。然而，这些历史人物与历史事件，又有谁去真正关注呢？

这阕词是词人第二次兼知建康府（今江苏省南京市）时，登镇江北固山有感而作。

宋人王灼认为叶梦得词“学东……得六七”；清人冯煦也认为他的词“挹苏氏之余波”。此词步苏轼名作《念奴娇·赤壁怀古》之韵，在构思和谋篇布局上，与东坡之词有颇多类似之处。

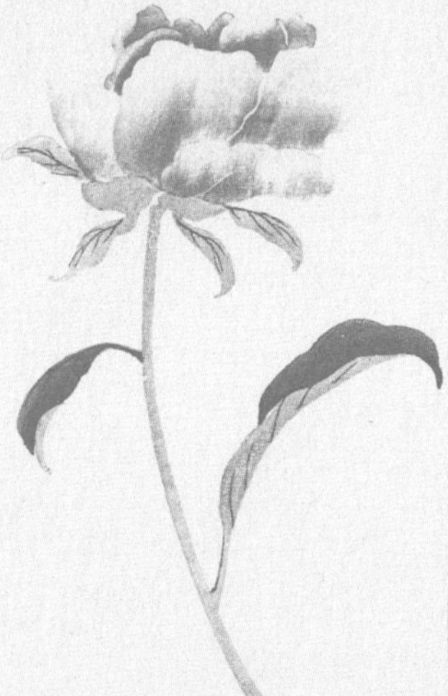

水调歌头·霜降碧天静

叶梦得

九月望日，与客习射西园，余偶病不能射，客较胜相先。将领岳德弓强二石五斗，连发三中的，观者皆惊，因作此词示坐客。前一夕大风，是日始寒。

霜降碧天静，秋事促西风。寒声隐地初听，中夜入梧桐。起瞰kàn高城回望，寥落关河千里，一醉与君同。叠鼓闹清晓，飞骑引雕弓。

岁将晚，客争笑，问衰翁。平生豪气安在？走马为谁雄？何似当筵虎士，挥手弦声响处，双雁落遥空。老矣真堪愧，回首望云中。

Prelude to Water Melody
Archery
Ye Mengde

Frost falls and quiet is the azure sky,
The west wind blows and hastens autumn high.
At first its song shivers me,
At midnight it enters the plane tree.
I rise to mount the city wall and gaze
To find mountains and rivers stretch for miles in haze.
What can I do
But to get drunk with you?
Drum beats on beats announce daylight,
The cavaliers bend their bow in flight.

The end of the year draws nigh,
In laughter guests would vie.
They ask me, old
If I can still be bold
As in days gone by.
Can I still ride my horse
And try my force?
Could I be like the archer who with ease
Would twang the string
With his fingers and bring
Down two wild geese
From the high sky?
I regret that old now. I cannot draw my bow
But turn my head to the northwest in the cloud
And long for heroes proud.

九月十五日，宾客们在西园练习射箭，我却因为偶然生病而不能一起参与练习，只好眼睁睁地看着客人以明显的优势领先取胜。岳德将领，弓的重量比二石五斗还要重，却仍能三发连中，观看的宾客无不异常吃惊，故而写下此词向诸位宾客展示。前一天晚上刮了大风，第二天就开始感觉到寒冷了。

九月霜降，碧天澄静，秋日里，西风又起。夜半时分，隐隐地听到窗外呼啸而过的寒风，正摇撼着落叶潇潇的梧桐。

强撑着病体，起身登上高高的城墙，向中原的方向望去，但见千里关河，甚是萧瑟寥落。国破山河碎，自是沉痛难耐，却只能借酒浇愁，拼着一醉，也要与诸君豪饮一番。战鼓声声，闹醒了清晓，练兵场上，骏马飞驰奔突，矫健的骑士个个拉满雕弓，此情此景，怎不让人心潮澎湃、振奋不已？

光阴易逝，年华已衰，诸位缘何都笑问我这白发苍苍的老翁，平生的豪气而今都去了哪里？我已经老了，血战沙场，纵横驰骋，谁才会成为真正的英雄？而今的我，怎么还能比得上席间诸位如龙似虎的猛士，挥手之间，弦声跟着响起，一箭便射落远处还在天上振翅翱翔的双雁？

年华老去，更兼体弱多病，再也无力报效朝廷，让我真心地感到无比的惭愧。但这并不代表我已经放弃了抗金的志向，要知道，我心心系念、时时回首遥望的方向，依然还是沦丧在金人铁蹄之下的北方故土。

宋高宗绍兴八年（1138 年），叶梦得再知建康府。九月望日，与幕下诸将操练弓箭，他因病而未能上场习射，更为自己年老力衰、无力报国，感到万分沮丧伤怀，便以此为主题写下了这阕词。

水调歌头·淮阴作

朱敦儒

当年五陵下，结客占春游。红缨翠带，谈笑跋bá马水西头。落日经过桃叶，不管插花归去，小袖挽人留。换酒春壶碧，脱帽醉青楼。楚云惊，陇水散，两漂流。如今憔悴，天涯何处可销忧。长揖飞鸿旧月，不知今夕烟水，都照几人愁。有泪看芳草，无路认西州。

Prelude to Water Melody
Written at Huaiyin

Zhu Dunru

In the capital then
We made merry in spring now and again.
With green belt and tassels red
We laughed and rode across the western river head.
At sunset we passed the ferry of peach leaves,
Flowers on head, we were retained by songstress' sleeves.
Green wine poured out from vernal pot,
Hats off, we got drunk in the blue tower. Why not?

The Southern cloud in fright,
The Northern river flows away,
Both drift in different ways.
But languid now,
Where on earth could I unknit my brow?
I salute the old moon with wild geese in flight,
Without knowing on whom she sheds her light
Across mist-veiled river tonight.
In tears I see lush fragrant grass,
But no way leads to Western State, alas!

遥想当年，洛阳城花团锦簇，春光明媚，少年们都喜欢成群结队地春游踏青，好不热闹。

身上穿着鲜艳的衣服，谈笑之间，不一会儿的工夫，就骑着马来到了城西的水边。日落西山，头上簪着鲜丽的花朵郊游归来，在经过渡口的时候，酒楼里的美人愣是上前留住了我们。

美人手持酒壶，一杯接一杯地劝我们饮下绿色的美酒。这样的殷勤，我们又如何能够推托，索性脱掉了帽子，开怀畅饮，直到醉卧酒楼，不省人事，自是快活得忘乎所以。

回首之间，狼烟四起，楚地风云惊变，陇水飘散而去，两地的百姓流离失所，各自漂流。而今，饱受流浪之苦的我，早已变得憔悴不堪，更找不到可以让我排遣内心忧愁的地方。

向着飞过头顶的鸿雁长长地作揖，只盼望它可以为我传来远方故人的消息。月亮还是曾经的那个月亮，现在，我只能一再地祈祷它，替我把祝福捎给共此一轮明月的亲人。

不知道，今夕里这迷蒙的烟水，都曾照过几人的离愁，只知道泪眼所见，唯有连天的芳草，却又牵惹出无限情思，而那条通往西州的道路，却是始终都遍寻不见。

宋钦宗靖康元年（1126年）十一月，金兵渡过黄河攻打洛阳，原是洛阳人的朱敦儒仓皇南下，加入哀鸿遍野的难民队伍，从此避难于淮阴（今江苏省淮安市）。遥望故土，回想当年情事，又值国破家亡，词人自是感慨万分，便在淮阴写下了这阕词。

朱敦儒（1081年—1159年），字希真，号岩壑老人，洛阳（今河南省洛阳市）人。早年隐居不仕，屡辞征召。宋高宗绍兴二年（1132年），赐进士出身，旋任浙东路提刑。后寓居嘉禾，晚年出为鸿胪少卿，有《樵歌》三卷存世。

喜迁莺·晋师胜淝上

李纲

长江千里。限南北、雪浪云涛无际。天险难逾，人谋克壮，索虏岂能吞噬。阿坚百万南牧，倏忽长驱吾地。破强敌，在谢公处画，从容颐指。奇伟。淝水上，八千戈甲，结阵当蛇豕(shǐ)。鞭弭(mǐ)周旋，旌旗麾动，坐却北军风靡。夜闻数声鸣鹤，尽道王师将至。延晋祚，庇烝民，周雅何曾专美。

Migrant Orioles
Victory on River Fei

Li Gang

The river a thousand miles long divides
The North from Southern land
By endless snowlike white-crested tides,
Impossible barrier set up by Heaven's hand
Strengthened by human forces,
Could it be crossed by Tartar horses?
The foe a million in strength
Fell on the south out of the sky.
But in a twinkling of the eye,
General Xie defeated them with ease, at length.

How great and strong!
On River Fei eight thousand spears in array
Defeated the giant swines and serpents long.
With whip in hand, and flags over the land.
They beat the foe as wind blows grass away.
Hearing the crane at night,
The foe, taking it for war cry, fled in fright.
They who prolonged the reign
And protected the land with might and main
Should be glorified by triumphant songs.

千里长江，一泻而下，雪浪滔滔，奔流不息，是阻隔南北江山的重要屏障。虽有天险可凭，但更为重要的还是人谋，如果有了深谋远虑，北方的宵小索虏，又岂敢吞噬我们的领土？

想当年，苻坚率领百万雄师渡河南下，一眨眼的工夫，便已深入我们的中原大地。大敌当前，大丞相谢安运筹帷幄，从容指挥，一战告捷，彻底将前秦君臣打回他们的老巢。

这场以少胜多、以弱胜强的战役，堪称伟大的奇迹。谢玄率领八千精兵，渡过淝水与苻坚的部队作战，阻止了像毒蛇和野猪一样凶残的敌人的进攻。挥鞭驾车前行，谢家军齐心协力，彻底击退秦军，旌旗飘扬之处，北军无不望风披靡。

苻坚登上寿阳城楼，极目远眺，已成惊弓之鸟的他，竟把八公山上的草木，都当作了严阵以待的晋军。败逃的路上，夜闻风声鹤唳，已经亡魂丧胆的他，也以为是晋军追杀了过来，一时间惊慌失措，弃甲曳兵，要多狼狈有多狼狈。

谢家军出奇制胜，力挫强敌，不仅保住了东晋江山，使中原大地免遭索虏吞噬，也使得百姓能够安居乐业。他们的丰功伟绩，哪怕是《大雅》《小雅》里所歌颂的周宣王征伐西戎、猃狁，使周朝得以中兴的事迹，也无法专美于前。

北宋被金国灭亡后，高宗赵构南渡，在临安建立了南宋政权。他满足于偏安于江左一隅，有志之士，无不为之扼腕，很多爱国文人都通过自己的作品，以多种手法表现了渡江北伐、恢复中原、驱除金虏、还都汴京的爱国热忱。

李纲感于时政，曾写有七阕咏史词。这七阕词的词牌和标题分别是《水龙吟·光武战昆阳》《念奴娇·汉武巡朔方》《喜迁莺·晋师胜淝上》《雨霖铃·明皇幸西蜀》《喜迁莺·真宗幸澶渊》《水龙吟·太宗临渭上》《念奴娇·宪宗平淮西》，而这阕便是其中之一。

李纲（1083 年—1140 年），字伯纪，号梁溪先生，北宋末、南宋初抗金名臣。祖籍福建邵武，祖父一代迁居常州无锡（今江苏省无锡市）。李纲能诗文，写有不少爱国篇章，亦能词，其咏史之作，形象鲜明生动，风格沉雄劲健。著有《梁溪先生文集》《靖康传信录》《梁溪词》。

六幺令·次韵和贺方回金陵怀古鄱阳席上作

李纲

长江千里，烟淡水云阔。歌沉玉树，古寺空有疏钟发。六代兴亡如梦，苒苒惊时月。兵戈凌灭。豪华销尽，几见银蟾自圆缺。

潮落潮生波渺，江树森如发。谁念迁客归来，老大伤名节。纵使岁寒途远，此志应难夺。高楼谁设。倚阑凝望，独立渔翁满江雪。

Song of the Green Waist

Li Gang

For miles and miles flows River Long,
Veiled in thin mist and cloud far and wide.
No more the captive's Jade Tree Song;
In vain old temple bell rang and sighed.
Like dreams Six Dynasties rose and fell fast,
Which would surprise the moon.
Gone are the wars and splendor of the past.
Who's seen the silver crescent wax and wane so soon?

The tides run up and down, the waves run far,
The riverside trees like thick hairs are.
Who cares for an old exile who came
Back wounded in fame?
Although the year is cold, the road is long.
How can I be deprived of my will strong!
I lean on rails in tower high
And look with longing eye
For lonely fisherman who fishes
Snow in the river as he wishes.

滚滚长江东流去，轻烟缭绕，水阔云低，自是壮丽非凡。陈后主创制的《玉树后庭花》，早已歌声沉寂，再也听不到了，耳畔响起的，唯有那古寺里敲响的稀疏的钟声，还悄然回荡在这千里长江的上空。

建都建康的六个朝代，一个接一个地覆灭，如同梦幻，倏忽惊了岁月，也惊了这无数的梦中人。兵戈的痕迹已经泯灭了，曾经的繁华豪奢也被一点一点地消磨殆尽，唯有天上的明月，纵使阅尽人间的盛衰兴废，照样年年月月，圆了又缺，缺了又圆。

潮起潮落，烟波浩渺，江边的树木茂密如发。屡屡遭到贬斥，身为迁客，有谁会怜惜我年华已老，还未能在抗金大业的道路上功成名就？哪怕边地严寒，我也要像松柏那样青苍挺拔，不畏冰雪侵凌；即便征途遥远，我也要把金人彻底赶出华夏大地。环境再险恶，时事再艰难，又有什么关系？我一定会坚持到底，矢志不移，任谁也无法改变我的心迹。

不知道是谁建起了这座高楼，凭栏凝望，而今的我，就像一个苍老的渔翁，孤单地怅立在江头。然，即便是披着这满身的江雪，我也要与侵略中原的金人决一死战，不达目的，誓不罢休。

这阕词，与词人于宋徽宗宣和三年（1121年）所写的《金陵怀古》诗四首，有某些类同之处，如："玉树歌沈月自圆""兵戈陵灭故城荒""豪华散灭城池古"。可以说，李纲的诗和他的词，在思想感情上有着异曲同工之妙，此词的语言风格也颇类诗，情感深沉，怀古伤今，低沉而郁发。

八声甘州·读诸葛武侯传

王质

过隆中、桑柘zhè倚斜阳，禾黍shǔ战悲风。世若无徐庶，更无庞统，沉了英雄。

本计东荆西益，观变取奇功。转尽青天粟，无路能通。

他日杂耕渭上，忽一星飞堕，万事成空。使一曹三马，云雨动蛟龙。看璀璨、

出师一表，照乾坤、牛斗气常冲。千年后，锦城相吊，遇草堂翁。

Eight Beats of Ganzhou Song On Reading Zhuge Liang' s Biography

Wang Zhi

When I pass by the premier's cot,
At sunset stand mulberry trees,
The millet struggles in sad breeze.
Were he not recommended by his peers,
How could the hero appear?
He planned to win over the east and west,
Of his career to reach the crest.
But with all the millet under the sky,
How could he build a way on high?

His soldiers tilled the ground by riverside,
But suddenly his star fell and he died.
Then all turned out in vain.
The three steeds became dragons in cloud and rain.
How glorious his plan to recover Northern plain!
His spirit rises high,
And shines in the blue sky.
After hundreds of years
The poet in the thatched hall still shed sad tears.

经过隆中的时候，放眼望去，桑木与柘木倚立在黄昏的斜阳下，绿油油的禾黍在秋风下不住地战栗，一派凄凉景象。

若没有徐庶的汲引，就一定不会有庞统的横空出世，像诸葛亮这样的英雄，也难免会被埋没于市井中。本来谋划要攻取荆州和益州，在帷幄中静观其变，等待将士们以出其不意的攻占方式建立奇功，没想到，在青色的庄稼地里转悠了一圈又一圈，到最后，竟然发现没有了道路。

当年在渭地屯兵的诸葛亮，终究还是像彗星一样突然陨落了，他一切的谋划，转瞬间，都成了一纸空谈。上天让北方的曹魏政权，和继曹魏之后兴起的司马氏家族，恰如蛟龙之逢云雨，顺顺当当地发展壮大，而汉中自诸葛亮去世后，便再也无力进举中原，恢复汉室。

尽管诸葛亮没有完成刘备去世前的遗愿，但一纸感人肺腑的《出师表》，却让他光耀千古，无人能及。即便是千年之后，还时时有人在成都凭吊他，而其中最为知名的，就要数以“草堂翁”自称的唐朝大诗人杜甫了。

这阕词的具体创作年份未知。王质读《三国志·蜀书·诸葛亮传》时，联想到自己郁郁不得志的身世，为表达内心的愤懑不平，便写下了此词。全词以叙事为主，间杂议论，只有开篇两句是景语，但读来流转自然，情寓理中。

王质（1135年—1189年），字景文，号雪山，其先东平（今山东省泰安市东平县）人，南渡后，徙兴国（今湖北省黄石市阳新县）。

游太学，与张孝祥父子交往，深见器重。绍兴中进士，辟为张浚都督江淮幕，入为太学正，被谗罢。虞允文宣抚川陕，辟为幕属。后入为敕令所删定官，又迁枢密院编修官。

虞允文荐质等三人鲠亮有文，可为谏官，亦为中贵所沮，出通判荆南府，改吉州，皆不赴。有《雪山集》四十卷传世，另《彊村丛书》辑有《雪山词》一卷。

八声甘州·故将军饮罢夜归来

辛弃疾

夜读《李广传》，不能寐。因念晁楚老、杨民瞻约同居山间，戏用李广事，赋以寄之。

故将军饮罢夜归来，长亭解雕鞍。恨灞陵醉尉，匆匆未识，桃李无言。射虎山横一骑，裂石响惊弦。落魄封侯事，岁晚田园。

谁向桑麻杜曲，要短衣匹马，移住南山？看风流慷慨，谈笑过残年。汉开边、功名万里，甚当时、健者也曾闲。纱窗外、斜风细雨，一阵轻寒。

Eight Beats of Ganzhou Song
On Reading General Li Guang's Biography
Xin Qiji

The Flying General was famed for his force.
When drunk, he came back at night,
At Long Pavilion unsaddled his horse.
But the officer drunk knew not the hero bright,
So the general stood without speech
Like plum or peach.
His galloping steed
Crossed the mountain in speed,
Taking a rock for a tiger, he twanged his string tight
And pierced the stone.
Not ennobled late in years, unknown,
He lived in countryside, alone.

Who would live in the fields with wine,
In short coat or on a horse fine,
And move to the foot of the southern hill?
Valiant and fervent still,
I'd pass in laughter the rest of my years.
On the thousand-mile-long frontiers,
How many generals won a name!
But the strongest was not ennobled with his fame.
Out of my window screen the slanting breeze
And drizzling rain would freeze.

夜读《李广传》，辗转不能成眠。因念及晁楚老、杨民瞻，曾相约同居山间，便引用李广的典故，写成此词寄给他们。

西汉大将军李广罢官期间，从田间夜饮归来，经过灞陵亭的时候下马宿营，却受到了喝醉酒的灞陵尉的欺辱。匆促之间，灞陵尉可能并未认出李广来，但名震天下的李将军，为人向来真诚笃实，受到众人的爱戴与尊敬，自然也就不会跟一个小小的灞陵尉计较了。

李将军曾单枪匹马地前往南山射猎，误把草丛里的石头当作老虎，弓弦刚刚拉开，就发出了惊天动地的响声，定睛一看，那箭镞居然射进了石头里，把石头都给射裂了。这样的英雄，竟没有受到封侯的礼遇，反而遭到了罢黜，怎不令人心寒？到了晚年，李将军索性退居山村，过起了耘田种菜的农家生活。

谁去杜曲种桑麻？反正我是不会去的。我要穿上轻便的短衣，骑上矫健的骏马，移居到南山，像李广那样潇洒落拓、慷慨激昂地度过余生，每一天都谈笑风生、心无挂碍。

汉代开边拓境的决策是英明而伟大的，很多豪杰都因此在长约万里的国境线上建立了不朽的功业。可为什么在非常需要人才的时候，像李广将军这样有胆略、有才干，而且又曾在边疆建立过奇功伟绩的人，却也落职闲居了呢？

我正在沉思的时候，纱窗外突地起风了，紧接着又淅沥淅沥地下起了绵绵细雨，朝屋里送来一阵轻寒。

这阕词写于淳熙十五年（1188年），作此词时，辛弃疾已经四十九岁。

辛弃疾二十一岁的时候就起兵抗金，南归以后亦多有建树，但因为人刚正不阿，敢于抨击邪恶势力，遭到朝中奸臣的忌恨，不仅未能实现恢复中原的理想，且被诬以种种罪名，在壮盛之年削除了官职。

他的这种遭遇，与西汉名将李广的生平极其相似，于是，便借此词倾诉了自己被无端落职、赋闲家居的悲愤心情，表达了对当权派倾轧忠良的不满，同时抒写了自己虽遭打击而意志终不衰退的豪情壮志，是典型的借古人酒杯，浇胸中块垒之作。

卜算子·漫兴

辛弃疾

千古李将军，夺得胡儿马。李蔡为人在下中，却是封侯者。

芸草去陈根，笕（jiǎn）竹添新瓦。万一朝家举力田，舍我其谁也。

Song of Divination
Random Thoughts

Xin Qiji

Long, long ago General Li was famed for his force,
Captive, he escaped by taking a Tartar horse.
Another Li was a man of common clay,
Yet he became minister ennobled in his day.

I mow the root of grass wet with dew,
And cleave bamboo to make tiles new.
If the court needed men to till the land,
I would be the best hand.

古代的李将军，受伤被俘后还能夺得匈奴人的骏马良驹，遗憾的是，功勋赫赫的他，不过官至太守。他的堂弟李蔡，人品在下中等，却被天子封为列侯，这是多么讽刺啊！

锄草要去掉老根，引水灌溉要先剖开竹子使成瓦状，这样才能除旧布新，解决积重难返的问题。唉，万一朝廷要推举努力耕田的人，除了我还能有谁呢？

小令以李广喻自己，指出像李广这样智勇双全的英雄人物，却总是被排斥迫害。对此，词人是极为愤慨的，但他却反话正说，不说自己的愤慨，偏说“举力田”，在“舍我其谁”的放达叙说中，表达了强烈的愤慨和对南宋朝廷的尖锐嘲讽。

阮郎归·耒阳道中为张处父推官赋

辛弃疾

山前灯火欲黄昏，山头来去云。
鹧鸪声里数家村，潇湘逢故人。
挥羽扇，整纶巾，少年鞍马尘。
如今憔悴赋招魂，儒冠多误身。

The Lovers' Return
Meeting a Friend on My Way to Luoyang

Xin Qiji

At the foot of the hills lamplights hasten nightfall;
Over the hills clouds come and go like a pall.
Passing the village, I hear the partridge's homesick song,
I'm glad to meet an old friend on my journey long.

Head covered with silk hood, a feather fan in hand,
While young, our steeds raised dust on the land.
Now languid, we're in spirits low,
The scholar's habit has brought us woe.

天色逐渐变得昏暗，山头飘浮着一朵朵倏忽来去的流云，抬头望望，已近黄昏。鹧鸪声声鸣叫的地方，掩藏着一个住着数户人家的村庄，而我却在这冷清的潇湘道上，意外地与故人相逢了。

也曾学着诸葛亮的模样，手执羽扇，头戴纶巾，镇定自若地指挥着千军万马与敌军鏖战，少年时代的我，是何等潇洒，何等有英雄气概！现如今，尽管已经憔悴落魄，但我依然要效仿宋玉，替那些在战场上失去生命、为大宋献出过宝贵青春的战士们，写就一篇《招魂赋》。而这，也是我唯一能为他们做的事情了。唉，自古以来，书生多是无用之辈，读了许多的书，到头来却误了自己的终身，怎不令人唏嘘惆怅。

宋孝宗淳熙三年（1176 年），词人由江西调任京西转运判官，第二年又调任江陵知府兼湖北安抚使，辗转一段时间后，更被调往湖南，仕途不可谓不坎坷，身世不可谓不漂泊。这阕词大约作于淳熙六年（1179 年）或淳熙七年（1180 年），此时词人正担任湖南转运副使和安抚使。

鹧鸪天·壮岁旌旗拥万夫

辛弃疾

有客慨然谈功名，因追念少年时事，戏作。

壮岁旌旗拥万夫，锦襜(chān)突骑渡江初。
燕兵夜娖(chuò)银胡䩮(lù)，汉箭朝飞金仆姑。
追往事，叹今吾，春风不染白髭(zī)须。
却将万字平戎策，换得东家种树书。

Partridges in the Sky

Xin Qiji

While young, beneath my flag I had ten thousand knights;
With these outfitted cavaliers I crossed the river.
The foe prepared their silver shafts during the nights;
During the days we shot arrows from golden quiver.

I can't call those days back
But sigh over my plight;
The vernal wind can't change my hair from white to black.
Since thwarted in my plan to recover the lost land,
I'd learn from neighbors how to plant fruit trees by hand.

有位客人慷慨激昂地谈论功名，我便回想起年轻时候的事，用游戏心态写下这首词。

我年轻的时候，曾举着旌旗，统率着一万多的士兵。战士们穿着鲜明的衣甲，跟着我英勇杀敌，冲破了敌人的重重包围，最终渡江南归。金兵在夜里枕着箭袋小心地防备着我们，却不料我军一早便万箭齐发，向他们的敌巢发起了进攻。

追忆往事，感叹而今的我年华渐老，即便是染绿世间万物的春风，也不能把我的白胡子染成黑色。叹，写了万字有余的洋洋洒洒的平定金虏、光复中土的方略，终是无人理睬，我只得拿它向东邻换取栽树种花的书，从此只做个安于现状的田园翁好了。

辛弃疾先后在各地做了二十多年的文武官吏，因进行练兵筹饷的活动，常常被言官弹劾，罢居在江西上饶铅山一带，也接近二十余年。他处处受到投降派的掣肘，报效国家的壮志终是难酬。这阕词则是他晚年居家时，和客人一同谈起建功立业的事，引发对自己人生经历的回顾而即兴所作。

柳梢青·岳阳楼

戴复古

袖剑飞吟。洞庭青草，秋水深深。万顷波光，岳阳楼上，一快披襟。

不须携酒登临。问有酒、何人共斟？变尽人间，君山一点，自古如今。

Willow Tips Green
Yueyang Tower

Dai Fugu

With sword in sleeve, I croon and fly
Over two lakes deep, deep in autumn dye.
Of Yueyang Tower from the height,
I see the vast expanse of rippling light,
The breeze affords me great delight.

I need not mount with wine;
I'd ask who'd drink with me and write verse fine.
The world has changed not the Queen's Isle
Seeing the past and present with a smile.

袖里藏着短剑，我自昂首歌吟，在洞庭湖和青草湖间来去自如，那明净而又浩瀚的秋水正不知有几许深。雄伟的岳阳楼上，我独立楼头，一边看着脚下的万顷波光，一边迎着西风敞开衣襟，快活得不能自已。

用不着携带美酒登临高楼，只需拈着一缕清风同行。我问你，就算带着美酒，又能与谁共斟？世间事，总是变幻莫测，唯有湖中露出一点的君山，依然故我地屹立在原地，自古至今都没有改变。

宋孝宗隆兴元年（1163年），宋金符离之战金国战败后，金国内部出现政变，无力继续南下侵宋。然而，南宋朝廷却没有利用大好形势规划北伐，恢复中土，一心只图苟安，在之后的数十年当中，双方都没有再发生战事。

南宋君臣长期沉溺于歌舞淫乐当中，词人虽远离官场，但却无时无刻不牢记着抗金复国大业，每当登临之际，爱国豪情就会油然而生，这阕词便是在这种情况下创作的。

戴复古（1167年—约1248年），字式之，自号石屏，天台黄岩（今浙江省台州市黄岩区）人。南宋诗人。不得功名，浪迹江湖，隐居于故乡南塘石屏山上。以诗享誉江湖间，为江湖派作家；亦工词，词风自然，豪健奔放。有《石屏诗集》《石屏词》存世。

满江红·赤壁怀古

戴复古

赤壁矶头，一番过、一番怀古。想当时，周郎年少，气吞区宇。万骑临江貔(pí)虎噪，千艘列炬(jù)鱼龙怒。卷长波、一鼓困曹瞒，今如许？江上渡，江边路。形胜地，兴亡处。览遗踪，胜读史书言语。几度东风吹世换，千年往事随潮去。问道傍、杨柳为谁春，摇金缕。

The River All Red
The Red Cliff

Dai Fugu

Passing the head of the Cliff Red,
Can I forget the bygone days,
When the young general spread his heroic rays?
Thousands of steeds roared like tigers by riverside;
Hundreds of ships in wrath with fish and dragon vied.
Rolling long wave on wave,
They beat the foe so brave.
What happens nowadays?

The ferry on the tide
And roads by riverside
Have witnessed all
Dynasties' rise and fall.
Seeing the relics of war,
We understand history all the more.
How many times has changed the world which raves!
A thousand years have passed away with the waves.
I ask the roadside willow trees:
"For whom are you swaying in vernal breeze?"

每次经过赤壁矶的时候，都会引发一番怀古悼今的思绪。想当年，周瑜年少有为，意气风发，气吞山河，威震寰宇。他率领着数万精兵驻扎在江边，擂起的战鼓震天响，手下的兵丁个个勇猛英武，发出的叫声像老虎的吼叫一样震慑人心。

千艘战舰上同时燃起了猛烈的火炬，那些平时潜居在江中的鱼龙，也因为受到战火的波及而变得怒不可遏。水面上卷起了长长的火龙，孙刘联军一鼓作气，将盛气凌人的曹操和他的大军团团围困住。俱往矣，一切都烟消云散，回头看看，现今的朝廷在和金人的角逐争斗中，又是副什么模样呢？

江上的渡口，江边的小路，全是地势险要的战略要地，也是当年两军对垒，一决生死的地方。亲眼看见这些历史遗迹，让我深切地感受到百闻不如一见，身临其境真的要比在书房里捧着历史书籍死记硬背强了许多。

东风吹，光景移，三国至今，已经改朝换代无数次了，千年往事也早就随着潮水滚滚逝去，不可再追。怅问道旁的杨柳，年年都是为谁萌发春枝，又是为谁一直摇曳着这嫩黄色的柳条？无论如何，感时伤世的我，的确是没有心思再欣赏这些曼妙的景致了。

这阕词作于宋宁宗嘉定十二年(1219年)左右，词人此时正在鄂州、黄州一带漫游。黄州城外有赤壁矶，又名赤鼻矾，传说是三国时期的古战场，词人过此，难免会引发思古之念，故写下了这篇《赤壁怀古》。

此词风格豪迈，雄浑有力，在娓娓道来的描述中，时有浓重之笔出现，于平淡中见奇伟。清人纪昀十分欣赏这阕词，认为它的豪壮之气并不逊于苏东坡的作品。

八声甘州·灵岩陪庾幕诸公游

吴文英

渺空烟四远，是何年、青天坠长星？幻苍崖云树，名娃金屋，残霸宫城。箭径酸风射眼，腻水染花腥。时靸（sǎ）双鸳响，廊叶秋声。

宫里吴王沉醉，倩五湖倦客，独钓醒醒。问苍波无语，华发奈山青。水涵空、阑干高处，送乱鸦斜日落渔汀。连呼酒、上琴台去，秋与云平。

Eight Beats of Ganzhou Song
Visiting Star Cliff

Wu Wenying

Mist spreads as far as sees the eye.
When did the big star fall from the blue sky?
It changed into a green cliff with cloudlike trees,
Where golden bowers were built for lady fair
In royal palace now in sad debris.
On Arrow Lane the eyes were hurt in chilly air
And water stained rouge with fallen flowers sweet.
Leaves fall on hollow ground;
'Tis autumn's sound;
It seems as if I heard the lady's slippered feet.

In royal palace drunk the king did lie,
But the tired hermit on the lake
Fished all alone awake.
In vain I ask the silent sky;
My hair turns grey in face of mountains green.
The sky is mirrored in water serene.
Leaning on railings high,
I see crows scatter on the beach in setting sun.
I ask for wine long and loud,
And stand upon Lute Terrace, where is none
But autumn high and lonely as a cloud.

灵岩山云烟缥缈，高峻雄阔，仿佛是天上的长星坠地而成，却又不知在何年何月。放眼望去，眼前这苍翠欲滴的山崖，葱茏蓊郁的云树，吴王夫差称雄天下的宫城，美人西施金屋藏娇的馆娃宫，还有那气吞山河的霸业，莫非都是幻化出的不成？

灵岩山前的采香径笔直犹如一支弓箭，凄冷的秋风吹得眼睛生疼，我几自走在古老的溪畔，那污腻的流水中仿佛还漂流着宫人们当年残留的脂粉，沾染得就连岸上的花朵都带了点腥味。耳边突地传来阵阵清脆的声响，却不知是美人西施穿着木屐走在响屧廊的余音，还是风吹落叶发出的飒飒之声。

深宫里的吴王夫差，终日沉醉于酒色之中，到最后落得个国破山河碎的悲惨结局。唯有头脑清醒的范蠡，辅佐越王勾践灭吴后，便即功成身退，从此泛舟五湖之上，好不逍遥恣意。

我想问问眼前这苍茫浩渺的水波，到底是什么力量主宰着历史的兴衰盛亡，它亦无法作答，只能以沉默回应。我思虑殆尽，愁绪纵横，满头白发苍苍，却无奈，那无情的群山依旧峰峦叠翠。

江水浩瀚，包含着无垠的长空，我独自凭倚栏杆，登高望远，但见几只飞不成列的乱鸦，正顶着夕阳的余晖，落在了水边捕鱼的沙洲上。置身于灵岩绝顶，无边的秋色和烟波浩渺的太湖美景尽收眼底，我连声呼唤同行的伙伴赶紧把美酒取来，快快登上琴台，去观赏秋光与云霄齐平的美景。

这是一阕怀古词，作于宋理宗绍定年间（1228年—1233年），词人其时正在苏州任仓幕。朱祖谋《梦窗词集小笺》引《吴郡志》："灵若山即古石鼓山，在吴县西三十里，上有吴娃宫、琴台、响屧廊。山前十里有采香径，横斜如卧箭。"吴文英通过凭吊吴宫古迹，叙述吴越争霸往事，寄托了古今兴亡之感和白发无成之根。

全词意境悠远，气势雄浑，情景交融，虚实相衬，清丽高雅，沉郁苍凉。吴文英改变了正常的思维方式，将常人眼中的实景化为虚幻，虚幻化为实景，通过奇特的艺术想象，创造出如梦如幻的艺术境界。

一萼红·登蓬莱阁有感

周密

步深幽。正云黄天淡，雪意未全休。鉴曲寒沙，茂林烟草，俯仰千古悠悠。岁华晚、飘零渐远，谁念我、同载五湖舟？磴古松斜，崖阴苔老，一片清愁。回首天涯归梦，几魂飞西浦，泪洒东州。故国山川，故园心眼，还似王粲登楼。①最负他、秦鬟妆镜，好江山、何事此时游！为唤狂吟老监，共赋消忧。

①最负他一作：最怜他

A Sprig of Reds On the Fairy Bower

Zhou Mi

Deeper and deeper I go,
When yellow clouds fly under the pale blue sky
And still it threatens snow.
In Mirror Lake the sand is cold,
In dense woods mist-veiled grasses feeze,
I look up and down for the woe thousand years old.
The year's late and turns grey,
I wander farther away.
Who would still float.
With me on five lakes the same boat?
By stone steps slant the old pine trees,
In the shade of the cliff old grows the moss;
Sad and drear, I am at a loss.

Turning my head from where I stand,
Could I not dream of my homeland?
How can I not shed tears for my compeers?
The mountains and rivers of the land lost,
How I long for my garden of flowers?
Could I not gaze back as the poet on the towers?
What I regret the most,
Is the fair Chignon mirrored on the Lake.
Should I revisit the land when my heart would break?
I would revive the fanatic poet old
To croon away the woe ice-cold.

山路曲折迂回，一步步登上幽深盘旋的小径，抬头望望，但见云霭凝重，天色昏黄，眼看着马上就要下雪了。鉴湖水澄澈依旧，寒沙凄冷，昔日繁盛的兰亭，而今已是断壁残垣，葳蕤的树木下，到处都是丛生的衰草，一派荒芜萧条的景象。

俯仰之间，悠悠岁月，千古往事，倏忽已成陈迹。叹我年华已老，飘零的足迹却是越走越远，不知道何处才是尽头。还能有谁顾念于我，愿意和我一起远远避开人世的离乱，同乘一叶扁舟，五湖游遍？繁华落尽，古老的石阶旁，唯余倾斜的古松，那山崖背阴之处更是布满了斑驳的青苔，四周都染遍了凄清的愁绪。

回首往事，孤身漂泊天涯的日子里，我曾无数次梦回西浦、泪洒东州。今日归来，本应心怀喜悦，却不料，待看到这故国的山川，故乡的田园，心里的悲伤，竟跟王粲当年登楼时的心绪别无二致。

黯淡的心情，终是辜负了秦鬟妆镜的美景。江山如此多娇，却遭到金人的肆意蹂躏，即便是故地重游，又为什么偏偏要选择在这个时候？罢了罢了，还是赶紧为我把那终日里都在鉴湖边溜达的疏狂酒徒贺知章叫来吧，我要与他一起把酒吟诗，一醉解千愁。

据王沂孙《淡黄柳》词序云：“又次冬（1276年）公瑾自剡还，执手聚别……敬赋此解。”按王词中所云“翠镜秦鬟钗别，同折幽芳怨摇落”诸语，可知周词亦为同一时间所作。该年正月，元兵攻入杭州，宋室灭亡，在故国沦亡的情况下，词人登临古阁，感慨万千，遂创作了这阕词。

图书在版编目（CIP）数据
锦里繁华 : 美得窒息的宋词 : 汉英对照 / 许渊冲译 ;
吴保阳解析. -- 武汉 : 长江文艺出版社, 2024.2
ISBN 978-7-5702-3293-2

Ⅰ.①锦··· Ⅱ.①许··· ②吴··· Ⅲ.①宋词-注释-汉、英
Ⅳ. ①I222.844

中国国家版本馆CIP数据核字(2023)第138937号

锦里繁华 : 美得窒息的宋词 : 汉英对照
JINLIFANHUA : MEI DE ZHIXI DE SONGCI : HANYING DUIZHAO

责任编辑：栾　喜　　　　责任校对：韩　雨
封面设计：棱角视觉　　　责任印制：张　涛

出版：长江出版传媒 | 长江文艺出版社
地址：武汉市雄楚大街 268 号　　　邮编：430070
发行：长江文艺出版社
北京时代华语国际传媒股份有限公司　（电话：010-83670231）
http：//www.cjlap.com
印刷：三河市宏图印务有限公司

开本：787毫米 × 1092毫米　1/32　　印张：8.5
版次：2024年2月第1版　　　2024年2月第1次印刷
字数：100千字

定价：49.80 元

版权所有，盗版必究
（图书如出现印装质量问题，请联系 010-83670231 进行调换）